"What does it look like...this black wall?"

"Death! It's a winding path with arms and legs. Its body is hinged inside the earth like a massive giant and it waits patiently for newcomers to come within reach; to lay eyes upon its grandeur. I've seen it one time and I don't want to see it again."

"Is it real or something you have manufactured?"

Ralph's demeanor sharpened. "What's the matter with you? It's real! Have you been sheltered all your life?"

I was becoming defensive. "No," I raised my voice. "I haven't been sheltered all my life. The question was valid. You were out of your head when Melissa heard you say it. She doesn't know what you meant; any more than I do. Either you want to talk about it or you don't. For once in your life, spit it out. I'm getting tired of pussy footing around with you." I stood up to leave when Ralph motioned for me to sit back down. I continued to stand.

The officer outside the door appeared. "What's the matter here?"

"Nothing, sir. It is ok. Ralph and I just had a meeting of the mind. We're fine." The officer shut the door and I sat down.

"Ok, Ralph, I want you to tell me about the black wall. I need to know and so does Melissa. Why were you writing your name?"

For the first time, Ralph's tense body melted into a soft repose. "The wall is real. If I remember correctly, there are 58,245 names on the wall. It includes 1,200 MIA's, POW's and a few others. It's the National Vietnam Veteran's Memorial in Washington, D.C."

Joyce L. Rapier

FULL CIRCLE

By Joyce L. Rapier

This is a work of fiction. The characters, incidents and dialogues in this book are of the author's imagination and are not to be construed as real. Any resemblance to actual events or persons, living or dead, is completely coincidental.

No part of this book may be reproduced or transmitted in any form or by any means, electronic or mechanical, including photocopying, recording, or by any information storage and retrieval system, without permission in writing from the publisher.

EZP Publishing
www.ezppublishing.com
A division of Champagne Enterprises
Copyright © 2006 by
ISBN 189726187X
November 2006
Cover Art © Chris Butts
Produced in Canada

EZP Publishing
#35069-4604 37 ST SW
Calgary, AB T3E 7C7
Canada

Dedication

To Tommy J. Moon, a wonderful American and Vietnam Veteran whose story touched my heart. Your sacrifices as an American soldier, through horrendous war scathing embattlement, should be applauded. This tribute is to you, because we, the people, as American citizens would not know the freedoms we have today. Thank you, Tommy for being an outstanding citizen and friend.

One

It's time for me to see Dad. Why it took me so long to make the drive is hard to comprehend but it doesn't matter now. Too many things have happened—some good, some bad, but it's time to let him know I understand. Thirty-seven years is a long time to come to grips with my insecurities. Stop lambasting yourself, Todd, you've been to see him...you just couldn't talk. Get on with it, get it done!

Wheeling my old car through the gates, the majestic presence of trees brought me to a time long ago when everything was perfect; playing base ball or shooting hoops through the make shift goal attached above the garage door. Horseshoes I could barely lift, a pretend canoe ride, climbing trees thinking it was centered at the top of the largest mountain on earth, paper airplanes and pirate hats, and hiding in mounds of freshly fallen leaves, was all I thought about when I was small.

Someone rubbing the top of my carrot topped head or ribbing me about freckles running together across the bridge of my nose didn't bother me. I would posture myself in defiance, grin and retort with the obvious reply, "Mom says I am handsome! I look just like my dad." Now, I'm forty-three and realize those memories were the most precious times spent with my dad.

Although my carrot top is bordering on salt and pepper, I did manage to lose the air of willful extremes. I was exuberant when I put away the God awful tortoise shell, horn rimmed glasses and chose the new and improved metal frames. At least my nerdish appearance faded...except for the plastic pen case in my shirt pocket. Some things never change. Oh, well, no one can go back to their childhood and revive useless wasted minutes or retrieve silent words, but the memories lodged in the mind transcends over all areas relative to change.

Jarred from my daydream by a tire sounding as if it exploded, I slowed my car to avoid repeated thuds from speed bumps. Stopping the car to see if a tire did go flat, nature revealed an awesome sight and trills. Astounded by the manicured lawn, I wanted to run barefoot though its dewy-kissed blades and feel the tickle between my toes. Vibrant yellow hues danced on the petals of daffodils and bright red tulips emitted a mesmerizing aroma. The crocus, dabbled among rock filled landscape, tweaked my imagination and essence of how small flowers know when to bloom. Birds, eager to procreate their species, chirped pleasant songs showing their way of greeting a new day and announcing the change of season. It seemed to be their way of telling me to slow down and enjoy life. I was in awe. Realizing there was no flat, I continued up the winding drive. Soon I approached the attendant in charge of the gated community.

"Hello, Todd. You're out early. It's 6:30 in the morning! I just barely had time enough to grab a cup of coffee." He nodded thoughtfully. "You've finally come for a visit. Your Dad's been waiting on you. The last time you were here was with your mom."

"Yes sir, I know, Mr. McGuire. I had too many things preying on my mind to stop and visit with him...now I do. It's a long over due visit. I can't say I am looking forward to it but there are so many things I need to tell him."

"You will do fine. Just speak what's in your heart." Mr. McGuire lowered his head and whispered, "But hey, Todd, don't be surprised if it's unusually quiet. Around here, people don't speak their minds."

I laughed, "I definitely won't be surprised, Mr. McGuire."

"Do you think you will be here long?"

"It depends on how quickly I can spill my guts to Dad. I have a lot of ground to cover and it may take awhile. It's why I came so early…to get everything pent up inside me…out."

"You have a captive audience, Todd. I don't think he will mind seeing you or listening to what you have to say."

"I just hope I can do it without breaking down. It sure has been a long time, Mr. McGuire. Do you think he will understand?"

"No question about it. A few tears never hurt anyone. When you keep tears from falling, it shuts off the natural instinct to heal. In my heart, I think he will love to see you. Go on now, go talk to your Dad. It will do both of you good. Especially you, Todd."

"Will you be here at your post when I leave?"

"This will be a busy day on the grounds and I probably won't go too far from my post, but if I'm not standing here, be sure and press the buzzer so I will know you have gone. I may be in my quarters but the computer scan lets me know when someone exits. The gate will lock automatically when you leave."

"Thanks, Mr. McGuire. I will do it. Have a good day."

"Good luck, Todd."

I waved at Mr. McGuire as I went down the narrow one lane road. He was a compassionate old gentleman full of advice for the hardest of hearts. I pulled into my intended area. The air was sharp with a north breeze. It curled around my face making me take deep breaths. Any minute I would see Dad. It didn't take long for me to approach him. I sat down on the bench and stared at the azure sky. I took a deep breath and wondered how to approach him and then blurted out the massive words bundled inside me.

"Hello, Dad. Please forgive me for not coming here sooner to have a long talk. You have to forgive me so I can forgive myself. It's been so many years but the fear inside me wouldn't allow me to approach you. Please, I know you can't talk to me. I will do the talking…you just listen. I've grown up Dad…into a man. I will never be the man you are, but you have given me more the last few weeks than you will ever know.

I want you to listen to some things…things happening recently bringing me closer to you than I ever thought possible. Sure, we had fun times when I was small and those memories are precious to me but being here now, is due to mom. If it wasn't for her, things might have been different…I may never have come to see you. It wasn't your fault, Dad, but my own insecurities. My life has veered down many roads, but I know mom has filled you in on all I have done or thought of doing and which road I finally chose. Many things I've done I'm not proud of, but for the most part, I can't complain.

I'm going to sit here beside you and spill my guts. I want you to know why I am here and the circumstances giving me the impetus to start this conversation. Roads have been crossed with people I have met but they are intertwined. They all have a purpose, sort of like a cake mix, Dad. Without one single person making me go in a clear direction, the other would not be meaningful. Bear with me, Dad, because as I progress in what I am telling you, it will become crystal clear. If I cry while I talk to you it's because my heart beams with pride knowing your bravery…you are my hero, Dad.

It might take awhile because I have a lot of ground to cover, but the story will eventually reveal a man whose life probably ran parallel to yours. You might have known him. His name is Tommy J. Moon. He told me some things…things you might have experienced, but before I tell you about him, you need to hear me out. Listen to me…please, because this is what has happened to bring me here today. It's going to be a long story. Several months ago, Mom came to see me. She waltzed right into the house..."

Two

"Boo! Gotcha'! I'll give you a penny for your thoughts."

"You want to give me a single little penny? I need a quarter! Good night nurse and little bitty fishes, Mom, you scared the hinkin', dinkin' daylights out of me. I didn't even hear the doorbell. How did you sneak in here without me hearing you? You have to stop doing it. I nearly knocked myself out hitting the blasted water pipes."

"Well, if I have told you once, I have told you ten thousand times; the stupid ringer doesn't work. You really need to get it fixed before an axe murderer comes in here and whacks you to pieces. I sure would hate to find you hanging from the rafters by your toenails. What the heck were you doing with your head under the kitchen sink?"

"I was trying to put a mouse trap under there. I've been fighting with a mouse the size of a football. The little goober runs through the house all night long chewing through wood and concrete. It has to have a stomach made of steel because it is gnawing all the time. One of these days, I will wake up and my house will be gone. The cake I brought home from Thanksgiving dinner on Thursday has mouse tracks all over it. I knew I should have put it in the fridge. It was my favorite cake, Mom!"

"Ah, a little mouse couldn't be as voracious as you were when you were a boy."

"But, Mom, it's my favorite. If I could get my hands on that furry little moocher..."

"Good grief, don't worry about the cake. I have more at the house. When it comes to eating cake, you still have a bottomless pit. I couldn't seem to fill your appetite. Remember?"

"Remember? Sure I remember. Wasn't anything better than your cooking...except for Kenny's mom's pickles. I haven't had a good pickle since she passed away."

"You mean to tell me my pickles weren't as good as hers?"

"Yeah, they were good. Kenny liked yours and I liked his mom's. We traded off. Don't look like the grim reaper has just visited you, Mom. I thought you knew."

Mom ruffled the top of my head with a quick swat. "Don't worry, I knew. I caught Kenny sneaking off with a quart of pickles and he told me...years ago. I thought it was funny. His mom knew what was going on, too. You kids could never keep secrets from us."

"I wonder what happened to Kenny. Funny isn't it how you lose track of friends you think will last forever?"

"Nothing lasts forever...not even friends. People go their separate ways, have families and grow up. It's not that they aren't your friend; you just grow apart. He may be thinking the same thing about you right now."

"Mom, you say strange things. Maybe I should look him up. Last time I heard, he was living in Monroe, Wisconsin."

"Call information and get his number. With a last name as unusual as Sevenstar, I can't imagine there would be more than one in the book."

"You're probably right." I looked out the kitchen window to see if it had started to rain as the weatherman predicted. Glancing at the old teapot clock above the sink, my brain kicked in. "What are you doing here, Mom? It's after six o'clock and dark outside. It's supposed to snow this evening. You should be home by now. You're never out this late. I worry about you because you know your eyesight is not the best."

"Oh my word, Todd, you're too much of a worry wart. I was going home from working on the church's Christmas bazaar and just needed to see you. Sometimes I start to think and well..."

"You're thinking about Dad, aren't you?"

"I guess I am."

"Mom, Dad has been gone for thirty-five years. I know it pains you to think about him. It does me too. It seems just like yesterday, but today is the anniversary of Dad's death. Are you going to the cemetery tomorrow; like always? If there is snow on the ground, I'll drive you."

"Do you honestly think I would forget the anniversary of your Dad's death? Yes, I'll go visit with him tomorrow and no, I will drive my own car, thank you!" Mom pulled out a chair and sat down. "You know, he could have been buried in the National Cemetery but told me never to do it. Before he left for boot camp, he made me promise to abide his decision."

"Why?"

"When we were going together, we would walk through the old cemeteries and trace the dates with a graphite pencil and notebook paper."

"Mom!"

"For crying out loud, Todd, we didn't raise the dead. We just found it fascinating; looking at history."

"You don't have any of those tracings lying around the house, do you? I wouldn't want to go over to your house and have ghosts coming after their dates."

"Don't be saying stuff like that, Todd. If you will be quiet for a few minutes and stop wise cracking, I'll tell you the answer."

"Okay, Mom, I promise to be a good little boy and stop giving you the business. Tell me why Dad made you promise."

"He always said it looked so lonely...not having flowers on the tombstones. It is such a stark sight to see all of the white stones in a row. It's so somber. You can't help but think about soldiers and their families. On Memorial and Veteran's Day I watch ceremonies on TV; American Flags flying and saluting the brave soldiers. I stand in awe of the beauty and what those soldiers did for our nation and I cry. Don't misunderstand, Todd, the National Cemeteries are beautiful but not for me. He knew I would pitch a fit not being able to put what I wanted by his side. It was his choice and I abided by his decision."

It was apparent Mom needed to talk but I tried to change the subject. "Mom, why didn't you ever remarry? You've been alone for so many years. I could have had a brother or sister."

Mom smiled at me, most likely realizing I was trying to change the direction of our conversation because we had been through this routine before in some testy conversations, but didn't rise to the bait. "I guess I couldn't find anyone to fill his shoes and besides, I was too busy trying to earn a living for the two of us. Some questions go both ways. I could ask you why you didn't remarry after your Betty passed away—but won't."

"Well, Mom, it appears as though neither of us could find anyone to fill their shoes. Wasn't Dad's Army pension enough to live on?" Seeing her dismay, and knowing I touched a raw nerve, I hugged her. "I'm sorry, Mom, I guess it was a stupid question. You wouldn't have had to work, would you?"

"Back in the sixties, Army pay wasn't what it is today. Nothing is what is used to be. I know the government thinks they know what's best for us, but any service man or woman should not have to worry about meager pay. Having a man or woman put their life on the front line should be more than what the Senators earn. Senators are up on the hill barking out orders, while at night they are home in a warm bed. They are supposed to be servants of the people but we wind up paying for their pensions while some of us go hungry. It doesn't include all the other perks they stick in their pockets or the enormous raises they give themselves. It's a travesty and something should be done about their greed."

"Ah, Mom, don't go there. You know you can't fight city hall or whatever the government does. They don't listen to what the public has to say. They make the rules; we pay!"

"Think about it, Todd. You pay more than you think. They buy a toilet or sink for thousands of dollars or pliers with gold plated handles…you pay for those things with your tax dollar. What happens if poor old JQ Public makes an honest mistake on taxes? Why, they are hauled off to jail, fined or put under a microscope…analyzed, chastised or hung out to dry. Most of the Senators are or have been lawyers and know how to pull strings. It's wrong—anyway you slice it—it's wrong!"

"Mom, don't get twisted in frenzy. I was just making a point."

"Dad blast it, Todd, your point does make me frenzied. If one of them had to go to war, they would be singing another tune. Only a hand full of them might know what it is like to do without…but I seriously doubt it. Not a cockeyed one of them would be willing to live as normal people having to make ends meet…wondering where their next penny would come from or how far it would have to be stretched."

"Didn't you and Dad have any savings?"

"Savings? Maybe a couple hundred dollars but it didn't last long. As far as your Dad's pension, yes, it helped for awhile, but bills piled up on me, just like all the other service families. I really didn't want to work, but it helped me forget the long empty days while you were at school. The nights were worse. I wouldn't have worked anywhere but you being in school all day, made me change my mind. Sometimes you have to do things you don't want to do. Work never hurt anyone…it keeps you on your toes. Old Doc. Crowder really didn't need a receptionist, but I guess he felt sorry for the two of us and hired me. He and your Dad were good friends, and he promised your Dad he would take care of us if something happened to him."

"He kept his promise, didn't he? Dad would have been proud knowing Doc. Crowder kept his word."

"Yes, he would—he would indeed."

"Mom, you're not the only one who thinks about Dad. Sometimes I wonder how things might have been had he not been killed in the war. Do you suppose Dad would have been the same—emotionally—if he came back home to us? Why in the world did he decide to join the Army?"

"He was drafted. He was considered 1-A, and had no choice about going. The draft was mandatory and if you didn't go, you were subject to arrest. It wasn't something he wanted to do but he loved this country. He would have never gone to Canada to avoid the draft; like some men did, skipping out to live in freedom while your father fought to keep them free. Thank God, the draft is no longer in existence. I hope in my lifetime war will cease but it's a pipedream. Your first question; I don't know. The horror stories I have heard of Vets returning home—I shudder to think. Some of the men never regain security. All wars prey on service men's minds. Killing leaves a gaping hole in the mind; knowing that taking a life is wrong. War is war; you kill or be killed. I'm sure your father's fear in killing someone, is no different from what the soldiers in Iraq feel today. In his heart, I believe your father would have been the same loving man I married but we will never know, now, will we?"

"I'm sure I have asked this question before but how exactly, was Dad killed? Up until now, I have managed all these years to block it from my mind. I haven't even visited his grave for fear I wouldn't say the right things. Don't ask me why, but with the raging war in Iraq, I need to know. Maybe I feel guilty about not ever having gone to war."

"Todd Jenkins, you know darn well you have been to the cemetery."

"Not to sit and talk to Dad. Sure I've been there with you but did you ever see me talk to him? No!"

"You just weren't ready to talk and you shouldn't feel guilty. I don't believe you would have been capable of going to war, not with your prosthesis. It wasn't meant to be. To visit your Dad, yes. Go to war, no."

Mother sat down at the kitchen table. Her eyes misted and a far away look shadowed her face. It was as though she was in a trance but continued, "How was your father killed? It is as fresh in my mind as it was when I was notified. I was told about choppers landing in a field close to the Ho Chi Minh Trail in Vietnam. The Ho Chi Minh Trail was deadly—God awful deadly. It was nothing more than a maze of jungle trails; used for the Communist troops as they moved from North Vietnam to get near Saigon to overthrow the government. The Ho Chi Minh Trail was used to carry supplies to the enemy. Anyway, to make my long story short, the chopper was there to pick up the wounded. All around them, mortar shells were firing at a rapid rate. Your Dad was lifting a wounded man onto the chopper, screaming to all the other soldiers to get down. A bullet hit him in the back. A medic on the chopper pulled him inside and did the best he could. They flew him and the other wounded men to the hospital, but it was too late. He died on board the chopper. I've always heard; you don't hear or feel the bullet that kills you. He earned a Purple Heart for his valor. It's too bad he didn't even know about it."

"I vaguely remember the chaplain coming to the house but then, I was only five years old. The old black cars lined up in the driveway and those men in their military attire scared me. The weather outside was just like today; overcast with rain."

"It was a bad day in our life but it happened. Life goes on."

"Do you think Dad would have taken up where he left off; being a tailor? I remember him taking measurements, chalking arm pits and joking with the men; telling them they needed to lose the pot belly. Then he would laugh—oh, how he could laugh. Some of the men weren't too happy to hear their weight was the cause of larger sizes."

"I can't answer something I don't know. I wouldn't suppose he would have returned to tailoring. The Boston Store, where he worked, closed. When they hired him, he was so excited. He came home, kissed me real hard and told me he was the new man in charge of the tailoring department. When he told me he would be sewing suits, I laughed my head off. Why, he couldn't even spell "tailoring" but he showed me a thing or two. He turned out to be a fine tailor."

"I don't remember the store. What was it like?"

"Well, you were too small to remember. I can recall going inside the department store to take him his lunch. It was grand; millinery racks, lingerie displays and outer-wear folded neatly between two pieces of white tissue paper, and stacked inside the glass shelves. At the time, saleladies would approach with a big smile and ask if they could assist the patrons. Today, there are no downtown stores to even step inside."

I smiled at Mom knowing I had her on a roll. Mom could talk a sign right off a butcher shop and it was good she was talking. Maybe it would help take her mind off Dad. "There are a lot of stores still downtown. I love those old stores…especially the junk stores."

Mom chuckled. "See there, even you admit the shops are mostly filled with junk. Some of them are good for the community, especially those re-sale shops through the Salvation Army. They actually do a service to needy people."

"What about the banks? They are downtown."

"You're trying to be a smarty pants, Todd. You know what I mean. I'm talking about clothing stores. The major stores have gone to the outskirts of town for one stop shopping. Clothing makers are fast pressed to manufacture in bulk and everyone dresses the same. Sometimes you can't tell a woman from a man."

"It's not so bad, Mom. It's the sign of the times."

"Good grief, Todd. The styles have changed so much; your Dad would be appalled. Men used to be dapper in suits and the women looked smart in dresses. Now, people are too relaxed and don't care what they wear. I never thought I would say this, but it would be nice to see a little more decorum, instead of seeing a man's shorts slipping down their backside; exposing the crack of their butts. Some of the women think it is proper to show off their breasts with clothing dipping down to their naval."

I laughed out loud at Mom's quip but she retorted, "But, my opinion doesn't count; I was brought up from the old school. I can't change the world or push my up-bringing on them. The world is changing way too fast for me to think about it now. What brought up this subject, anyway?"

"When I start to think about Dad, I am reminded of Patch Dimple. Patch Dimple was my hero—like Roy Rogers or The Lone Ranger. Dad made him my hero by telling me it was okay to talk to an inanimate object. Patch Dimple never let me down. He was there when Dad wasn't."

"Patch Dimple? I haven't heard you speak his name for years. How does he remind you of your Dad?"

"For awhile, I couldn't bring myself to think about Dad; dying like he did so far away. It cut like a knife through my heart to think he was alone; fighting the war in Nam, dodging all the napalm and hidden traps. I will never forget his last words to me when he got on the old green bus, heading for boot camp. He said, "Todd, you have to be the man of the house while I am gone. Don't let your Mom run roughshod over you. While I am gone, don't be tearing this thing apart; you know your Mom can't sew." Then he laughed and handed me Patch Dimple. Patch Dimple was the ugliest thing I ever did see but Dad fixed him up. He had been patched so many times; Dad swore another patch would do him in. After he left, I would pick up Patch Dimple, squeeze him, put him up to my face and smell Dad's Old Spice cologne. Mom, I want to come by your house and get Patch Dimple. Is he still in the attic?

"Todd, you know Patch Dimple was sold in our garage sale."

"Sold? Oh, Mom, no! A lock of Dad's hair and letters he sent me was in Patch Dimple. I read all the letters but was too young to grasp Vietnam; let alone, understand what he was saying. By the time I went to college, the thought of Patch Dimple was not forefront on my mind. Getting my degree was all I could think about. Now, as I have gotten older, I want to re-read all the letters he sent to me. It's the only thing I have left of Dad. *I can't tell her Dad's Purple Heart is inside Patch Dimple. Oh, God, please...please help me find Patch Dimple.*"

"I'm sorry, Todd. I had no idea you put the letters inside Patch Dimple. You told me I could sell him. Don't you remember? We needed the money when your Dad died and the garage sale was the only thing at the time, to get money to pay the utility bills."

"Do you remember who bought him? Think, Mom. He was inside an old tin box. I have got to find Patch Dimple."

"Todd, it was so many years ago. Some of the neighbors came by and bought things...but I don't remember. What I didn't sell, I gave to the Salvation Army. A few mementos you wouldn't allow me to sell are stored in the attic. Why don't you come by tomorrow and go through the stuff? Maybe Patch Dimple is still up there. I have to go to the church tomorrow and work on the bazaar. If I am not home, just use your key and take what you want. I don't have any use for it; it's yours. There are bits and pieces of airplanes, baseball cards and other keepers; waiting on you to take them...like you should have when you moved out. It's just gathering dust. Gosh, look at the time. It's a quarter till nine. It's really dark outside. I had better be on my way home."

"Mom, let me drive you home. The roads could be getting slick. It worries me when you drive in the dark."

"Don't be silly. Who would drive you home? We'd be driving each other home all night long and never get anywhere."

I laughed and gave Mom the look; a look she knew all too well. "Mom, you'd better..."

"You don't have to finish the sentence. Yes, I'll give you a call when I get there. I know you don't like me being out past dark. Old bones aren't what they used to be and neither are my eyes. Before you ask me the next question; my cataract surgery is scheduled for the first week in January."

"You took the words right out of my mouth. Don't forget! Now, come here and give me a hug and kiss. You know, Mom, I love you more than anything in this world. I don't know what I would do without you."

"I love you, too, Honey."

"Don't forget to phone me when you get home."

"I promise. It's the first thing I will do when I get there. Bye, Sweetie, love you bunches."

"Bye...and don't be sneaking up on me again, you hear?"

Mom laughed. "Okay."

Three

It was cold outside and snow was falling at a rapid rate. Dark clouds hovered like spirits waiting to sheath me with emptiness. Ice was adhering on tree branches and my heart felt the cold chill; like fingers piercing my soul, digging away at my being. All I wanted to do was sleep. Forget the past two days; erase them like a child wiping chalk marks from a dusty blackboard. Silence was unbearable; food tasted like cardboard. Alone...the awful word alone...echoed inside my mind. For the first time in my life—I was alone! The doorbell rang; I tried to ignore the sound. *Go away! I don't want to see anyone.* It rang again and I made my way down the hallway and opened the front door.

"May I help you?"
"Does Todd Jenkins live here?"
"Yes, I'm Todd Jenkins."
"I know you probably don't remember me, but do you mind if I come in for awhile. I'm Mrs. John Wilkins...Charlotte, a friend of your mother, Thelma. I was a neighbor of your family. We lived in the two story house on Vine Street; next door to the old Presbyterian

Church...the one turned into a library. You do remember me, don't you?"

"Mrs. Wilkins, it's been awhile since I last saw you but sure, I remember you. Your daughter's names were Melissa and Julie. Melissa and I used to sneak in the old church and ring the tower bell. It's a shame it had to be torn down. Come on in. You shouldn't be out in this cold. You've heard, haven't you? Bad news travels fast, doesn't it?"

"Yes, I've heard and hoped and prayed it wasn't true. I had to come see you. The women at the church sent this tray of food to you. I know it isn't food you want right now but maybe—maybe tomorrow you will see the need for it. More of the congregation will be by tomorrow. This snow has put a damper on some of the ladies venturing outside. We're not as young as we used to be. The ladies' sent this card to you...we all signed it. Is there anything we can do for you?"

"I appreciate the food, Mrs. Wilkins and I know Mom would be thankful someone is looking out for me."

"This is such a sad time for all of us, Todd. Your mother brought so much pleasure to all of us. I...I just don't know what to say."

"I understand, Mrs. Wilkins. It's all such a blur to me and right now...I don't know what to say to you, either."

"Has the service been set? Reverend Whitley said to tell you he will be by here after this evening's service and help you with the eulogy. I don't think the Sunday service will last too long with the weather getting so bad. This early snowfall has us old folks in a dither. The preacher said to tell you prayers would be lifted up and he would phone before coming here."

"The service can't be held until Tuesday afternoon. The funeral home told me the florists are closed on the weekends and flower service couldn't resume till early

Monday morning. Although I don't understand it, I would have preferred to have the service yesterday, but I guess there are those who would like to put flowers near her casket. Mrs. Wilkins, you'll have to forgive me. I don't even know what I am saying. I'm just rambling."

"You don't have to explain it to me. I have been in your shoes and understand how you feel. Mr. Wilkins died on a Friday evening, too. If you don't mind me asking, what happened? I am not being nosy...we loved her."

"I'm not too clear about the accident. You all must have known Mom's eyesight was not the best, but she couldn't bring herself to stay home at night. We had a battle and she relented to getting her cataracts removed. Her appointment was the first of the year. I begged her to let me drive her...anywhere she wanted to go, but her stubbornness won out. The times I did drive her where she wanted to go was like pulling teeth. She was so independent and the thought of not driving sent her over the edge."

"We tried to do the same thing...tried to convince her to let us drive. She wouldn't hear of it. Mind you, we aren't in the best of health and she would remind us of the fact. It's not your fault, Todd."

"I know it's not but I still feel, somehow, I could have prevented it from happening. The Old Grist Mill road, one block from her house, was under repair, and..."

Mrs. Wilkins interrupted, "It's an awful road. I don't know why the city hasn't fixed it sooner. With all the taxes we pay, a body would think they could afford to fix all the deep pot-holes to prevent this thing from happening."

"It's not the city's fault the accident happened. A culvert caved way from the rain and Mom's car went flying through the air. It was one of those freak accidents. There were no skid marks. The police said she apparently was going under the speed limit but probably didn't see the barricade. When she left here, it was raining and I guess the rain prevented her from seeing the amber flashers. When the police got to the scene, her car was upside down in the ditch. The driver's side window was shattered but she didn't have a scratch on her...not one scratch. Mrs. Wilkins, they think she might have had a heart attack. We won't know for sure until the autopsy reports come back to the coroner. The road crew had a flashing barricade around it but who knows."

"You know something, Todd? Friday afternoon, your mom was acting strange while she was working on the bazaar items. She would stop every few minutes, cough and take a deep breath. We saw her rubbing her arm but she told us it was nothing. We overheard her talking to your father. It wasn't a whisper; she was talking out loud to him. Her comment to us was to mind our own business...she was having quality time with him. Before she left the church, she told us she had an errand to run. It was close to 5:00 p.m. and she was frantic to leave. She said something about the store closing before she could get there. She flew out of the room as though it was on fire."

"Mrs. Wilkins, Friday evening was the anniversary of my father's death. Mom probably needed to get some flowers for his grave. Believe me; she wouldn't even go to the cemetery without flowers. She came by here after working at the bazaar and without question; he was on her mind. Maybe she knew her death was imminent. I've heard of things like this happening."

"How old was she, Todd?"

"She wasn't old; just sixty-three. She would have been sixty-four come January."

"Sixty-three! She was much younger than I expected. Why, I sure thought she was much older."

"Mom thought young, but her arthritis played havoc on her body. Some days she could hardly walk but her spunk made her move whether her body wanted to or not."

"Todd, take it from me, getting old is for the birds. Our minds think we are still sixteen but our bodies tell us differently. It would be wonderful if we could bottle up our energy at sixteen and save it for a rainy day at seventy."

I burst into tears. "My, Lord! I just thought of something. How could I have been so careless? Dad's birthday is tomorrow. When I was small, Mom would hold up his picture telling him she would, one of these days, see him on his birthday. God, I hated this time of year and now I hate it more."

Mrs. Wilkins put her arm around my shoulder. "Go ahead and cry, Todd. I'll cry with you. You must not blame this time of year for the things happening. Awful things happen each day of the year. We all go through times of sorrow."

"Mrs. Wilkins, for the longest time when I was small, this time of the year was not a happy time. Dad died two days after Thanksgiving and it left a bitter taste in my mouth. Having his birthday fall so close to his death made the holiday's worse. This year's Thanksgiving was no different from the first…it was empty. Mom and I always had a good meal but that's all it was. Now, it's started all over again. The only reason she was out so late is because she was working on the Christmas bazaar. Now Christmas won't even be the same. She and I would go together to get each other a special present and we'd sneak it in each other's house and make a game of it. It won't happen this year—it won't ever happen again."

We sat at the kitchen table pouring over years of memories. Tears flowed like a waterfall as we remembered each good deed and gesture she shared with those she loved. Our coffee cooled as we stared into space, thinking of things to say. We must have gone through six pots of coffee; not tasting a single drop. It was ten minutes past twelve and I needed to go to the funeral home to see Mom. I was just about to tell Mrs. Wilkins when she said, "I just heard my daughter honk the car horn. I'm sorry, Todd, but it's time for me to go. Melissa told me she would be here to pick me up after the church services. She was afraid for me to drive."

"I understand. You don't have to explain. Just a minute and I will walk to you to the car. The sidewalk is slippery from the snow. Wait right here until I get my coat."

"You don't have to bother, Todd. I can manage."

"Please, Mrs. Wilkins, this is something I need to do."

I put on my coat and escorted Mrs. Wilkins to the van. Melissa said her condolences and they drove away. It would be a long day; even though half of the day was gone. Walking back into the kitchen I placed the coffee cups in the sink and un-plugged the coffee maker. I couldn't delay going to the funeral home.

On my drive to pay my respects and take care of funeral arrangements, the route took me past the culvert where Mom died. I hadn't planned on stopping but my curiosity was more than I had anticipated. Snow had covered part of the culvert making it hard to see how Mom's car plowed through the barricade.

As I stepped from the car, my footing caught the edge of the metal sawhorse jutting up from the dirt and sent me reeling down the embankment. I slid ten feet, landing on the icy water beneath the snow. I could feel my heart racing knowing Mom must have felt the same way. Fighting the ground to secure my footing, I thought I saw something move. Adjusting my eyes to the glare of the snow, I bent forward and looked into the darkened crevice. At first I thought it was a field rat but I was wrong.

Beneath the shelter of the culvert lay a small German Shepherd puppy; not more than a couple of months old. She must have crawled under a sheath of metal to stay warm. Reaching down to pick her up, I noticed blood on her front paw. Shivering and whining she cuddled next to my chest with the ease of a new born baby. I was soaked to the bone and cold from the exertion, but I knew this little puppy needed medical attention and I raced to my car.

Searching through the trunk of my car, I pulled out a piece of chamois and wrapped the puppy snuggly inside. Cranking up the heater to stave off shivers, we raced down the slippery street to find the nearest veterinarian. *Oh, God, this is Sunday. Everything is closed for the week-end. What on earth can I do? I need to take care of Mom's arrangements. There's no time to go back home but I've got to do something before this puppy dies from exposure. Why is this happening to me? I have to go see Mom.*

I pulled the car into the funeral home parking lot and walked to the front door; puppy inside my shirt. The sign on the door read: Ring bell for service. Visitors use side door. I rang the bell and waited for what seemed to be ten minutes. A neatly dressed old gentleman opened the door, patted me on the back and told me to follow him. I am sure he was wondering why I looked so unkempt with wet and muddy clothes. He didn't say a word. He escorted me to a family room and said someone would be with me shortly.

Another long ten minutes passed before a tall, lanky, neatly attired director approached his desk. Even though he didn't comment on my appearance, his eyes wandered up and down my stance. I apologized for my disheveled attire and told him who I was. We shook hands and sat down; he on his Mahogany, plush velvet upholstered straight back chair and I on the matching antique twin; totally uncomfortable to say the least.

He began to fill out necessary forms, while I answered unending questions sounding like who's who in People's magazine. I wanted to scream out loud that these questions were too much, but I composed myself and continued. Actually, I was amazed to have remembered given and maiden names of Mom's parents. My hand shook as I signed the dotted line, affirming everything I knew to be true. It was overwhelming and so final.

As I stood up to leave, the puppy whose warm body had relaxed and curled under my arm, let out a yelp and howled like a banshee on the loose. The peaceful and solemn funeral home turned into a noisy, free for all frenzy. A stuffy, prim and proper woman at the front desk, whose eyes could slice through steel if you made a noise, followed suit with her own little tirade. Before I knew what was happening, the entire staff was standing in front of me wanting to know if I was dying. All I could do was open my shirt. Out popped the puppy's head and I explained the situation.

Atmosphere soon changed. Those people's attitudes, I thought to be stuffed shirts, turned into mounds of putty as they petted the head of my new found friend. Lucky for the puppy and me, the director had gotten his minor degree as a veterinarian and agreed to check the little puppy's paw. He cleaned and bandaged the wound, and told me to keep my mouth shut or he could lose his license as a mortician. The puppy couldn't talk so I made a vow for the two of us. I kept the promise.

When I got home from the funeral parlor, I fed the puppy and placed her inside a box. She would sleep while I continued the horrible task at hand—a task necessary to complete Mom's arrangement. It was the thing I dreaded most; going to Mom's house to get burial attire.

Pulling into her driveway was frightening. The house seemed to frown; sending out vibes chilling me to the bone. I turned the key in the lock and stood in the entry way for a long time. It was strange not having Mom come to the door to greet me, and I had the horrid sensation of someone looking over my shoulder.

Memories flooded over me and the emotional trauma shattered me into a whimpering mass. I felt like a thief rummaging inside Mom's house; looking through her closet for a dress and inside her bureau for personal lingerie. I selected one of her favorite suits, black pumps and matching jewelry. On the way out of her room, a small bottle of pink fingernail polish seemed to jump into my hand. Maybe it was an afterthought in completing her final appearance.

Locking the door, I made my way back to the funeral home to complete the final preparations. Monday, I would see Mom for the very last time, dressed in her finest as she lay in wait; prepared for her ultimate journey.

Tuesday afternoon, the small funeral home was packed with those attending the service. The family area consisted of one person—me. Before the service began, Mrs. Wilkins, her daughters, Melissa and Julie and two grandchildren joined me in the family room. I was relieved to know someone was thinking about me and understanding the torture surging through my mind and body.

The service didn't last long and we made our long ride to the cemetery. Cars lined up in a neat little row and slowly moved down the ice and sand caked streets. Actually, the drive was only three miles long but felt like an eternity. Even in the elements, cars were backed up for miles; headlights glowing through falling snow; like perfect halos reflecting sunlight on prisms. I had no idea Mom knew so many people—people of all ages, willing to be there for her passage.

Reverend Whitley was a God-send, saying and doing all the right things and soon, people were leaving. Exhaust fumes filled the freezing air as I watched the last vehicle leave the arched, gated columns surrounding the quiet burial ground. Twenty minutes after the last car exited, I told the driver of the family car not to wait any longer; I wanted to walk home. He shook my hand and drove away.

The stark reality of Mom never walking in my kitchen, the scent of her sweet perfume not lingering in my house and not being able to feel her hugs and kisses made me cry out in anguish. I stood alone in the silence of spirits, wondering why things had to have such an abrupt ending. An hour later, with no more tears to shed, I walked home. As I walked up the sidewalk, I realized I wasn't alone, I had the puppy. We had each other.

Four

Christmas came and went. My normal routine would be putting away all the decorations but there was nothing to put away. If all the Christmas trees in the world sat on my front yard with sparkling lights and tinsel, I still couldn't be enticed to embark on retrieving my decorations from the storage shed. It wasn't Christmas; it was depressing. The only thing keeping me from sheer insanity was my puppy, Patches, my new friend and companion.

After her paw healed, I could count on her to be right there, under my feet. Something about Patches reminded me of Patch Dimple; a scruffy, mottled Teddy Bear with a patch across one eye, gangly legs and feet the size of baseballs. Since I no longer had Patch Dimple, Patches would take the place of a long lost memory. I loved Patches and she knew it.

Being an accountant gave me something to do. Tax season was upon us and plowing through all of my client's receipts kept me busy. An occasional phone call would shatter my concentration and leave me in a foul mood. Thoughts of Mom clashed with crunching numbers and I could feel my insides grind and agitate. It was hard to come to grips with my emotional turmoil. Nothing could top the ache in my gut.

The television blared with commercials; sound raging at will. I grabbed the remote to turn it off but stopped dead in my tracks. I flipped the channels, one after the other, frantically trying to figure out if I actually heard what I heard. All the news channels were reporting the same thing.

"Headline News: December 26, 2004, an earthquake of magnitude proportions occurred off the west coast of Northern Sumatra. Seismologists report at 7:58:53 AM (local time at epicenter), a 9.0 earthquake erupted in the middle of the Indian Ocean. The mega-thrust occurred on the interface of the India and Burma Plates: caused by releasing stresses developing as the India plate sub-ducts beneath the overriding Burma plate. The force of the earthquake created a Tsunami, spilling waves thirty or more feet onto the shores of Sumatra, Sri Lanka, Thailand, Somalia, Tanzania, Bangladesh and other small countries lying in its wake."

I was horror-struck with the news. My mind could not fathom the actual size of the Tsunami. News of the deaths crushed my attentiveness toward my clients and I focused solely on each news report. It was all the same. Pictures of the Tsunami were slowly hitting the airwaves. Ravenous waves shot across the television screen; the Tsunami plowing through once beautiful shorelines, reducing and erasing them into oblivion. The waves appeared like enormous sharks, hungry for another blood thirsty round of mayhem; unwilling to be satisfied with a single prey.

I watched in dismay as debris clashed against waves of despair. Devastation was at an all time high; bodies lying in make-shift morgues, children crying out in fear, boats capsized while shards of wood hammered the shoreline. Electrical lines down, no drinkable water and food would be scarce. Diseases lay in wait to devour the remaining survivors. Without medical attention to thwart off malaria and other deadly diseases, what would these people do?

These once loving families gone; generations killed in a single natural disaster. I sat in my chair, glued to every word vocalized by the news media. I cried.

The reality of it all crushed me to the bone. It looked like a war zone without manmade bombs. Pandemonium was rampant and rightfully so. Twenty thousand persons dead; the count rising. Some reports indicated the death count could rise above one hundred thousand; probably more. The insanity of it, how people so unaware of the impending doom could go on with their lives, and pick up millions of shattered pieces appearing as Humpty Dumpty flailing as he fell from the wall, was beyond my wildest imagination.

My emotions vulnerable, I wiped the tears from my eyes and clicked off my television. Here I was, feeling sorry for myself and having a pity-party because of my mom's death. Shame on me! How could I be so callous with my self centered emotions? Those people lost everything...not just one family member but entire generations. Enough was enough. It was time for me to make a change in my life and move forward. I might not be able to do much, but I would try and do my part. My plan wouldn't take long to make it come to fruition.

Probate for Mom's estate went without a hitch. The normal six months waiting period to expunge debts didn't apply, since I was the only living relative. Mom's attorney, her financial advisor and I went over all of her personal accounts, putting things in order and paying any outstanding bills. Reluctant but knowing the job was at hand, I liquefied her personal real property. All assets in her portfolio came to me. I chose to transfer some of the money into my personal bank account and rollover a portion of the stocks. My inheritance wasn't enormous but I chose to give a portion of Mother's estate to the Tsunami victims. Mom's attorney handled the donation and made sure it was channeled to the proper source.

The next several weeks, I concentrated fully on my client's tax forms; doing paperwork, getting signatures and necessary payments due, and mailing the dreaded forms to the proper state and federal departments. Putting aside personal distractions, I tackled the enormous task glaring me in the face. It was time to clean out Mom's house. It would be a mountainous job deciding what to discard, sell, keep or give away. Knowing her the way I did, there would be tons of objects. I needed help for this massive project, but wasn't sure where to turn. I decided to put a help wanted ad in the newspaper.

As luck would have it, persons inquiring to the ad were not willing to have a part time job. It wasn't worth their while to work two or three hours a day. They needed a full time job. Some told me it would be exciting to rummage through all of her things and I quickly put an end to their exuberance. A few of the women inquirers told me they would have to bring their children. I loved children but didn't want to baby-sit some giggly little kid or wonder what they stuck in their pockets. Numerous potty breaks or time out's to eat wouldn't cut it. I tried not to be rude with my reasons, so I simply told them no. In desperation, I picked up the phone and cancelled the Saturday ad. It was becoming too much of a hassle. Out of the clear blue sky, the phone rang. I thought it was a client with a last minute tax revision.

"Good afternoon, Todd Jenkins speaking."
"Todd, this is Melissa Garner."
"Who?"
"I am Charlotte Wilkins daughter."

My mouth dried. I couldn't garner enough spit to swallow dry air. It felt like the Sahara Desert, as I knew—I knew immediately who was speaking to me. "You mean Mrs. Wilkins daughter? Gosh, I didn't even know you were married."

"Actually, I am divorced. I didn't think you would remember me by my married name. I sat with you at your Mother's funeral."

"Oh, I know who you are. The last name threw me. Sorry." *Shame on you, Todd. You know darn well her last name is Garner.*

"It's ok. I haven't been back here too long and a lot of people don't recognize who I am. Years have changed me."

"What may I do for you, Melissa?"

"Nothing in particular. I had you on my mind and thought I would see how you are doing. I would have phoned sooner but I knew you were not in a frame of mind to talk."

"You would have been right. Things are better now and my world is slowly getting back to normal."

"Are you up to company?"

"Well, yeah, I suppose so. Most of my clients have phoned, mailed or brought by their w2 information. I am pretty well caught up on the early birds. Some will wait till the last minute and yell for help."

"Clients? Talking about w2's, you must be a CPA. Maybe I shouldn't bother you right now. It sounds like you are too busy for company."

"I didn't realize until hearing it from you but CPA sounds so formal. Let's put it this way; I am an accountant. It's easier on the ears."

"Why don't I take a rain-check? Maybe we can get together later when you're not so swamped."

"No." I blurted out. "I would love some company. I am knee deep in trying to figure out what to do with Mom's personal belongings and stuck in limbo. I don't know in which direction to turn."

"Do you need any help?"

"Help? Did you say help? I would gladly welcome some help. Are you offering?"

"Sure."

"The pay isn't much; minimum wage."

"I'm not worried about pay. Being paid didn't even cross my mind. Todd, I was offering free help. You do know what the word "free" means don't you?"

My spirits soared and I kept my excitement to a minimum. "When can you start?"

"How about tomorrow morning?"

My heart was pounding so hard, I was sure she could hear the beats. "Sounds great. Would you like to grab some breakfast? We could go to the diner or I could scramble eggs. You make the call."

"Breakfast sounds wonderful. I tell you what...you get the coffee brewing and I will make the breakfast. What time would you like for me to come over?"

"I'm an early bird. How about 6:30 a.m.? Is it too early for you?"

"No. We can eat and then start house cleaning."

"Great. I look forward to seeing you again."

"I'll be there around 6:15. Bye."

"Bye." I hung up the phone and did a once over of my messy house. *Good grief, look at this place.* I let out a shriek and danced around the room.

Patches stared at me like I had lost my marbles. She cocked her head in bewilderment, as I cocked my head back at her. She knew what was next. Toenails tried to grip the hard wood floor and the race was on; an area rug would, as usual, go reeling through the air. Patches had grown so much she could barely fit under the end tables but had no trouble up-ending select items when we played. It was a given.

The game she loved best was to extract her favorite, chewed to bits rubber ball from a latched tin box. She would grasp the container firmly between her teeth and fling it against the wall. One way or another she managed to open the lid, snatch the ball and run from me. It was almost as though she was telling me, "You crazy human. Don't you know we four legged critters are smarter than you?" More than once, her playful romp sent the container into a blazing fireplace. She would sit in front of the fireplace and howl at the top of her lungs until I rescued the box from the flames. I had more blisters on my fingers than I cared to think about and swore it would never happen again. A secure fitting fireplace screen soon prevented first degree burns and alleviated smelling the stench of melted rubber.

After our usual play time, the messy house was still there. Not being married, single to do as I pleased, I was accustomed to my surroundings. Having magazines piled in a corner or newspapers strewn about the house didn't bother me. Mom ignored my idiosyncratic living as she knew I hated cleaning. Mind you, it wasn't always this way. I thought about Betty.

My deceased wife, Betty, was a clean freak; scowling at a dust bunny having the nerve to hide under a chair. We were germ free. An almost sterile atmospheric environment whistled up your nose leaving a taste of antiseptic adhering to the tongue. Sometimes I would gasp for air when she manhandled ammonia, Lysol or other cleaning supplies. It was my clue to leave the premises. For the longest time, after she died, I yearned to smell the horrid aftermath.

Betty and I met in college. I was a senior attending Oklahoma State University. We met by accident and I do mean accident. My digs were off campus; a run down two-story, gray dilapidated office building turned apartment house. With single units it catered to those who could not afford luxury. It was almost funny watching men scramble to secure a place in line for the single bathroom. It was the pits but we couldn't complain. I suppose I could have done better but each penny I earned from my part time job was spent on tuition or food. Sure, I partied. What normal college student doesn't party? Finding money for parties, didn't count...it was for parties, not tuition.

All the roomies had the same objective. Come Friday night we would crash together in one small room; for the usual beer and raising hell routine. Some Friday nights we would do the town; half cocked, and hell bent for leather to find trouble. It found us without too much effort.

There was, on occasion, a dastardly little deed called "hammer the boxes" using, of all things, baseball bats. It's a wonder none of was killed with the shenanigans we pulled or put under the local jail house; never mind a cell. I won't elaborate the meaning of "hammer the boxes" but will say it's one of the stupidest things I ever attempted. Once was enough for me and to this day I feel the affects of "hammer the boxes" reprisal.

We loaded as many guys into a car as it would hold without flattening the tires. Off we went, down the streets as though we had good sense. Never mind the cost. What could possibly happen? Seniors don't get hurt; they believe they are invincible. Wrong! Speed (not drugs) was the factor. Squealing tires in pursuit of fun dictated our focus. Perhaps learning the hard way was a lesson I needed.

We finished our night on the town. The driver wheeled the car into the apartment house drive way and the guys crawled out of the car. However, our apartment house was across the street. The idiot driver was smashed out of his head and didn't know one driveway from another. Not to worry, we would dash across the street, dodging honking vehicles.

Drunk as skunks and reeling from the excitement, we managed to put the baseball bats we had with us inside our pant legs. It was a damned stupid thing to do, but when you are three sheets to the wind you are not capable of making a clear decision. All of us were walking stiff legged, knowing if we got caught it would be apparent as to what we had been doing. Word had spread like wildfire and our escapades were becoming as transparent as Scotch Tape. Even through my stupor, I vowed this night would be my last time to participate in pranks unbecoming to this soon to be accountant.

Four of the men managed to cross the street without any trouble. I was lagging the group, jerking the ball bat up from my ankle. Each wobbling step I took made the bat slide down my pant legs. Things didn't go quite as planned. I wound up in the emergency room at our local hospital. How I got there was a miracle because I don't recall a thing. My mind was blank. I was told later, how and why my extremity would no longer be the same.

Several days later, awake from the aftermath of emergency surgery, realism hit me like a ton of bricks. I didn't know if I wanted to live or die, but a voice kept me from leaping out the third-story window. Hell, I couldn't have moved even if I wanted to. I was strapped down with so many tubes, wires and gadgets; I would have killed myself simply trying to get off the bed. I thought of drowning myself with the pitcher of water by my bed, but hell, I had to have assistance in sipping a single drop of water. On one attempt in reaching my glass of water, my agonizing screams brought all the nurses running into my room. I had pulled an IV needle from my arm and blood squirted in random directions. I needed to escape…escape or die damn it. From myself, this room and everything around me because all I could see was half a man.

"Oh, God!" I screamed out His name with unending questions until the breath in me was barely audible. I wasn't the same man I remembered seeing two weeks ago. Part of me was gone…cut off and discarded like it never existed. Dying would be a pleasure because I couldn't believe what I was seeing. My leg...my leg was gone. And due to the quick thinking nurses, my futile attempt to do self harm came to an end as well.

Depression was trying its damnedest to send me into a black hole—a never ending chasm. All I could think about was never playing soccer or skiing down a slope. Basketball, football or any other sport wouldn't be a part of my life. Life I enjoyed was longer an option; it came to an abrupt ending.

My sweet angel Mom was there each day and tried to make me happy. I could tell she was crushed; knowing her decision for amputation would forever change my life. Each time she entered the room, her happy smile would fade into creases of saddened eyes. Seeing her age right before my eyes; added to my depression. I don't know which was worse; knowing I was a cripple or seeing Mom so worn and hurt. I was the reason for her sadness, the reason for a gigantic hospital bill, the reason I was a cripple, the reason I might not graduate.

God, I hated what was happening and hated God for letting it happen. Why me, God? Don't you have enough to do without making me so miserable? I pounded on the sides of the bed screaming at God, cursing every breath I took. It was the worst nightmare a person could ever have but it wasn't a nightmare, it was real. Looking back, I can see there was no alternative. It was the only decision she could make.

After several weeks, despising my lower extremity pulled higher than my head, it was time for me to sit upright. The blood, surging downward through re-routed blood vessels, was like having a sixty ton elephant sitting on your chest. It reminded me of pinched air being released through a deflating balloon, screaming for an escape. My heart palpitated so hard, I knew any minute it would pound right out of my chest. The pressure inside my head was excruciating and the sound of anyone speaking turned into amplified speakers with the volume as loud as it would go. At times, I felt dizzy, shaky and nauseous. Having physical therapy was gruesome. I couldn't stand up-right without assistance and the pain rising and falling through my body made me scream in agonizing wails. Phantom pain was impossible to describe. I couldn't stand to see the throbbing muscles and bare nerve endings as the bandages were changed. Bloody raw flesh, even through stitches made me heave. My leg was ugly—simply ugly.

Physically forced to stand, by an aggressive physical therapist, I had to gain lost muscle tone in my good leg. The pressure, created from metal crutches gouging into my weakened arm pits, made the flesh of my arms ache. Yes, I was a cripple, half legged and doomed to life as an outcast. For what? An hours' worth of dangerous fun? God, how I wished to roll back the last several weeks and erase the pain I subjected myself to so that I could graduate with my classmates.

Betty entered my room at 6:00 a.m. I heard muffled voices between the doctor and Betty. They were going over my chart, flipping pages, one right after the other. The noise generated from the ball point pen scratching the paper grated on my nerves. It angered me to be jolted from sleep. All I wanted was to be left alone.

I could feel the bristle of a slight breeze as she passed my bed. Calmly, she walked to the window and opened the curtains. The sound of window blinds flipping upward incensed me. I became more hostile and deliberately back-handed the water pitcher. It crashed into the wall sending water splashing onto her uniform. Betty was as cool and calm as a sliced cucumber. She picked up the pitcher, placed it on the food tray and quietly looked at me.

In a monotone voice she snickered, "My, aren't we in a snit today."

Her voice took me off guard and I stared at her. I retorted, "Listen, bitch, we are not a "we." Understand? If I want to be in a snit, I'll be in a snit."

"Have it your way. Go ahead, have a little fit. I don't care if you come unglued. You are my patient, like it or not. I am here for the duration of my nurses training. If you don't like it, you can lump it. With or without you as a patient, I will get my degree. So, knock off with the attitude. If you're not careful, I will hit you in the head with a bed pan."

For the first time in a long while, I laughed. None of the hospital personnel had the nerve to spout back at me. I guess they all felt sorry for me or wanted to avoid getting the wrath of my anger.

I watched her closely. Her blonde hair was pinned up under her white cap. Large blue eyes glared at me, daring me to say another word. Her crisp white uniform and white stockings formed her body beautifully; making her the image of an angel. I thought I had died in my sleep and gone to heaven. Those thoughts quickly changed when I remembered cursing God.

I couldn't take my eyes off her for fear she was a figment of my imagination. She was beautiful; a figure of liquid movement, poetry in motion. Afraid she would disintegrate right before my eyes, I hoped she would come closer to my bedside. I needed to make sure she was real. My wish suddenly turned into catastrophic fear as she eased closer to my bed nonchalantly lifting the sheets from my partially nude body. Embarrassment overtook me and I hit the sheet to prevent her from seeing me.

Daggers shot from her blue eyes. "Just what do you think you are doing?"

"Listen, Lady, I am nude under here." I snapped holding down the sheet and defending my territory.

"So what? Do you think you have something special hidden under the sheet that I haven't seen before? I will guarantee you, I have seen it all."

You don't understand, lady. Right now, it is a BIG deal. Blushing beet red, I defended my stance. "Not mine you haven't!"

Betty gritted her teeth and hissed, "Don't make me jerk the entire sheet off you. I'll do it, you know."

Cold chills went all over me and everything under the sheet died as quickly as it arose. The white sheet went flying across the end of the bed and I lay there as passive as a baby. Everything on me shriveled so fast that I didn't have time to think. This tiny little woman scared the hell out of me. She meant business!

While she was washing my private parts, I shoved the pillow across my head. I couldn't look at her and I hoped nothing on my body had the urge to stand up and salute. I held my breath as long as I could until she lifted the edge of the pillow and said, "See. It wasn't so bad. You were worried for nothing."

I looked down toward my "Willie," grinned and breathed a sigh of relief. She knew why my sheepish grin crept across my face but said nothing. The hot sweat I had experienced dissipated and I allowed her to continue with the task at hand; changing the bandage on my stump. With her by my side, the gruesome ordeal was not so bad. Funny isn't it, how a person can waltz into your life and make things so much better? Betty did it for me. Just when you think you are boss, someone comes along and changes your mind. From then on, having Betty as my nurse would change my world in a way I thought could never happen.

For the next several weeks, Betty was at my side, lifting my spirits and making me regain my own self respect. She forced me to do things I hated, like maneuvering myself down the corridor in a large wheeled contraption for old people; telling me it was my own decision to stay in it or learn how to get along without it.

She taught me how to move on crutches, an art I didn't know existed. She was there, holding my hand when the first prosthesis was fitted to my leg. Always patient with me, always telling me I could do it. It was like having my own private nurse but I knew she had other patients and I was jealous. I couldn't bear to think she was as tender to other men as she was to me. I hated it when her shift ended and raised hell with the replacement nurse. It was torture having a wimpy nurse look at me and run for help. My attitude toward the evening shift was purely nasty but it wasn't them, it was me. I secretly wanted Betty.

All things had to come to an end. It was time for me to leave the hospital. Lucky for me, the university allowed me to continue my studies while in a hospital bed and I got my degree. I didn't know at the time, this procedure was not the norm. The vast majority of universities or colleges didn't give squat whether you managed to graduate; it was not their responsibility to be nurse maid or hold a student's hand.

It was Betty's doing. She approached the dean, told him the circumstances, said she would be responsible for making me study and the rest is history. I probably would never have found out what Betty had done if Mom hadn't accidentally let the cat out of the bag.

I didn't "walk" in the graduation ceremony with my classmates but I did get my sheepskin. All of this, I owed to Betty. While she was getting her degree in nursing, she was quizzing me for my final exams. In all honesty, she should have been honored for doing two things at a time-getting my degree and hers. I thought leaving the hospital would be the end of Betty and me but it wasn't the end, only the beginning.

~ * ~

Thoughts of Betty were interrupted by the sound of my hall clock chiming midnight. I hadn't cleaned up one single pile of papers and Patches was waiting on me to go to bed. Then I remembered Melissa coming to breakfast at 6:15 in the morning. I shoved papers into a hall closet, ran a dust mop across the floor, hit the toilet bowl with a brush and called it a night. Patches and I would forget about cleaning anything. We were ready for bed.

Five

The doorbell rang out and Melissa waited for Todd to come to the door. She rang the bell again and waited. Finally in desperation, a good swift pound on the door shattered the slumbering duo.

"Patches, quit barking! I'm trying to sleep?" *Good grief, who's making all the racket? It's enough to wake the dead.* I made my way to the front door and grumbled. "Who is it?"

"Todd, it's me, Melissa. Will you open the door or should I go back home?" she snapped.

"Oh, Lord!" *What the hell am I going to do? She can't see me in my birthday suit.* "Hang on a minute, Melissa. I think my commode is overflowing."

"What? At least open the door. This sack is getting heavy."

"Wait a minute, I said!"

"Well, stick it in your ear. I'm out of here."

Easing open the door, with hair sticking out in all directions and yesterday's shirt wrapped around my bottom, I sheepishly grinned. "Hi, Melissa."

"Hello? 6:15? Should I leave? What the hell happened to you?"

"Normally I am up at the crack of dawn. To be honest with you, I overslept. If Patches hadn't started barking, I might have slept till noon."

"I thought you said you are an early bird?"

"I am...well, not today though. We didn't get to bed until after midnight. I guess the alarm didn't go off. Will you excuse me so I can get some clothes on? The kitchen is to your left."

Anxious to extract myself from showing Melissa my birthday suit, I quickly made an about face in the direction of the bathroom. In my haste, the crutch fell to the floor, forcing me to hop on one foot the remainder of the way. My shirt fell to the floor exposing my rear end. I was embarrassed.

Melissa yelled at the bathroom door. "You know, Todd, we don't have to have breakfast. I can come back later."

"No, it's okay. Don't leave. I won't be but just a few minutes. Why don't you go on in the kitchen and start the coffee?"

Melissa was beginning to wonder why she didn't turn around and walk out the front door. She stood in the kitchen and stomped her foot. *This is the stupidest thing I have ever done. Here I am, trying to be nice to Todd and he is not even in the kitchen. He wasn't even awake. The butt-hole. I won't do this again.* She was just about to tell Todd she would be back later when he came up behind her.

"Melissa, you're a sweetheart to stay. I am so sorry I wasn't up. Will you forgive my laziness?"

"This time I will but I won't do it again." Melissa walked to the fridge and took out the eggs. Turning around to ask where the skillet was, she saw Todd attaching his prosthetic device. "Oh my God! What happened to you?"

"Didn't you see me hobble to the bathroom?"

"No, I was too busy wrestling with the sack of stuff I brought. The sack came apart and I was retrieving things that fell on the porch. It's a good thing I didn't have eggs in the bag or we might have a bacon sandwich for breakfast. By the way, Todd, I think I should tell you, your stupid door bell doesn't work."

"Yeah, I know it doesn't work. Mom told me the same thing. Hang on a minute while I fix Patches a bowl of food and then I will tell you about my leg."

While Melissa prepared breakfast, I asked, "Are you sure you want to hear about it before we eat? It's not pleasant."

"It won't bother me. I am a registered nurse."

"What? You're kidding."

"I have been a nurse for several years. It couldn't be any worse than what I have already been subjected to. Tell me all about it."

"It happened when I was at OSU."

"You went to OSU? So did I. Well, for awhile until I decided to go into nursing. I did take night classes for extra credits.

"I was there in 1984."

"So was I," Melissa shouted, eyes widening with the discovery. "It was you, wasn't it? You were the one hit by the car. I would have never made the connections. I had absolutely no idea it was you."

"Unfortunately, yes. Due to the accident, I kept a low profile. Not because I was ashamed but for the fact, I couldn't walk." I chuckled. "Sounds pretty stupid, doesn't it? If you don't have but one good leg, you can't walk, can you?"

"You have a point. No pun intended."

"The pun was funny because I do have a pointed leg. Hey, I just thought of something. You might have known my wife, Betty. She was in nurses training the same time you were. Her name was Betty Simpkins."

"I knew of Betty. I didn't know her personally, but many of my acquaintances said she was one of the best nurses ever to graduate. I often wondered what happened to her."

"She married me. If it hadn't been for Betty, I might have committed suicide. Man, I was in a bad way."

"Well, are you going to tell me how it happened?"

"Yeah, it doesn't bother me to talk about it anymore. A bunch of my drunken friends and I had been out on Friday night. We had been playing "hammer the boxes."

Melissa frowned. "Don't tell me you were among the ones doing the hammering? I know all about the pranks. It's a wonder some of them didn't wind up with severed arms."

"The first time I did it, was the last. It's the night I lost my leg. We were across the street from our apartment, trying to dodge traffic..."

"Wait a minute. Why were you across the street?" Melissa inquired curiously.

"The nut driving the car thought he was in our driveway. We were too drunk to have common sense. Anyway, the ball bat I had hidden inside my pant leg kept moving up and down. I stopped in the middle of the street to pull it up and the car hit me. The handle of the bat was at the calf of my leg. When the car plowed into me, it hit the handle and shattered the lower portion of my leg. People thought my foot flew off, but it was my shoe. It landed in the bushes; my foot dangled. The bones were so crushed, they couldn't tell where the ball bat began and my leg stopped. The impact, on the bat handle by my leg, thrust the upper portion of the bat through my trousers. It ripped off my clothes. I had bruises the entire length of my left side. Amputation was the only option. If that wasn't enough, I had broken ribs and a fractured hip. It's a wonder I didn't die from blood clots."

"How horrible. You must have been in terrible pain."

"It was awful but it woke me up in a hurry. It's the last time I took a drop of liquor."

"Todd, maybe this is a personal question and if you don't want to answer, I will understand. Where is Betty? Are you still married?"

"I am married to a ghost and the memories she left behind."

Melissa looked quizzical. "I don't understand. Was it a bad marriage, like mine?"

"It certainly wasn't a bad marriage. Betty was my soul mate and I loved her to death. We were made for each other but something came between us. Cancer."

Melissa's eyes glanced toward the plate on the table as to avoid eye contact with Todd. "I'm sorry, Todd. It was a personal question. I shouldn't have asked."

I stood from my chair and began clearing the dirty dishes. "You know something, Melissa? For the longest time, I felt my life had been shattered when Betty was diagnosed. It was like my heart had been cut from my chest. Never in my dreams, did I think something so drastic could cut short our lives together."

"What type of cancer did she have?"

"It was ovarian cancer. Betty and I tried to have a family but each time she conceived, she would have a miscarriage. We could never understand why her body was rejecting the fetus. Finally, she and I decided to see a specialist in fertility. We did all the right things at the right times. She had check ups, the whole nine yards."

"With Betty being a nurse, I can't imagine her not recognizing the symptoms."

"Oh, she had symptoms but neither one of us thought cancer. Bloating with gas can happen to anyone and besides, the symptoms of ovarian cancer can mimic normal aches and pains right down to constipation. It's just not something you think can happen to you."

"What happened?"

"One day she came home from work, exhausted. She had been tired before but this day was different. She could barely get from the car to the house. Her face was ashen and her stomach was swelling. We rushed to the hospital where they did tests. That's when she was diagnosed. Unfortunately by the time we found out, the cancer had ravaged her body. Biopsies yielded cancer in her liver, kidneys, lungs, and surrounded her heart. Surgery wasn't even possible. We cried, screamed, went to different doctors but to no avail. Nothing could be done. Her normal weight was falling so fast; clothes went from a size ten to four in a matter of weeks."

"You both must have been devastated."

"Devastated seems like a simple word but there is no other word to describe how we felt. We were in a state of shock. It's like being thrown into a freezer with no escape. You sit there, staring at a white, frozen wall knowing you have nowhere to turn. We cried millions of tears, pounded the walls with our fists, cursed and threw things, but it only created a vacuum."

"How on earth did you two manage to get through the ordeal?"

"One day at a time. We simply took one day at a time and tried to live it to its fullest. Sometimes the seconds skipped past so rapidly it turned into dark days. When Betty got to the point of needing round the clock care, she made me take her to the hospital. We fought because I wanted her here but I realized fighting was making her lose ground fast. She refused any type of machines except the electrocardiograph. She wanted us to know when she straight lined."

"How long was she hospitalized?"

"One week, two days, twelve hours and sixteen minutes. My Betty simply went to sleep. It was the end."

Melissa walked over to Todd and put her arms around his neck. They stood embraced for several minutes, not knowing what to say. Melissa whispered, "Todd, I am so sorry."

They jolted when Patches flung her rubber ball against the wall. "What in thunder was that?" Melissa screamed.

I laughed. "It's Patches. She wants to go outside." Patches' tail was wagging like a pendulum on a clock; barking frantically to tell her master she wanted out.

"You scared the daylights out of me, Patches." Melissa said, as she bent forward to rub the back of Patches ears. "Todd," Melissa posed, "I've seen this dog before. I'm not sure where, but she is sure familiar. Where did you get her?"

"It's not possible. I found this little puppy on Sunday after my mother passed away. She was under the culvert where the accident happened. She has been with me from then till now."

"How strange. I know I have seen her face somewhere. It's so unusual, with the patch over her eyes. She looks like a raccoon. Maybe I am imagining things; couldn't be her."

Patches came bouncing inside the house. "Look at this face, Melissa. Now you know why I named her Patches. She could be a double for my Patch Dimple."

"A who? What is a Patch Dimple? I know you told me you stopped drinking but did you scotch your coffee?" Melissa laughed. "What a funny word--Patch Dimple."

"It's not funny! Patch Dimple was my faithful teddy bear. When I was small, Dad had patched him so many times; stitches covered stitches."

Melissa walked into the living room. "This I have to see. Where is Patch Dimple?"

"Long gone, sold to the highest bidder, in a garage sale. Hey, look at the time. If we are going to start cleaning the house, we'd better be on our way. Leave the dishes, I'll do them later. By the way, breakfast was wonderful. You're a good cook."

We stacked the dishes in the sink and made our way to the house. The drive was pleasant but it was because I had someone with me. It had been a long time since a female sat in the passenger seat of my car and it felt nice. I could smell the faintness of her perfume but hesitated to tell her I enjoyed the delicate fragrance. I didn't want to sound dorky or come off as a typical male. Besides, this was a working arrangement and would only last until Mom's house was liquidated. It was stupid of me to think otherwise but I did— I did.

Melissa broke the silence as we pulled into the driveway. "Gosh, Todd, this house is smaller than I remembered. I recall running through hedges trying to catch footballs. The yard doesn't seem as big either."

"Don't forget, we're all grown up. Most objects are larger when you're small. Mom had the hedges removed when the police caught a burglar hiding inside them years ago. The thief had burgled several neighbors before they found his hiding place. She came unglued knowing the hedge was his safe haven. The next day, after he was arrested, she was out here with a shovel trying to dig them up. After fighting with the roots, she gave up and called Mr. Whitsett. He fired up a small backhoe and in a matter of minutes, the hedges were history."

"Do you remember when your mom took the water hose and sprayed the two of us for fighting? I will never forget the look on your face when the water shot up your nose."

"It nearly choked me to death. You were laughing and Mom was chasing me. She got a kick out of showing us who was boss. Do you remember why we were fighting?"

"Vaguely. You had come up behind me and twisted my head."

"Is it all you remember?"

Melissa thought for a few seconds. "Todd Jenkins, you were trying to kiss me, weren't you? By golly, you were! I didn't realize it until now."

"I sure as heck didn't have any luck. After I got up enough nerve to kiss you, you screamed. Boy, I was so mad, I didn't care if I ever kissed you. I was so embarrassed. When the water hit me, all I wanted to do was run and hide. I sure cooled off in a hurry. Oh well, it's in the past and I don't have to worry about getting doused with another water hose. Come on. Let's see how much house cleaning we can get done."

We walked inside the house, giving it a once over. In unison we said, "Where do we begin."

"Where are the boxes, Todd?"

"What boxes?"

"Boxes to put stuff in or did you just want to throw it outside in the yard?

"Heck, I didn't even think about boxes. Now what will we do?"

"Don't get all bent out of shape. Let's take one room at a time. Let's start in the kitchen. While you are going through things; I'll drive to the grocery store and get some banana boxes. Be sure to make a pile of trash, things to give away and things to keep. Hand me your car keys and get with it."

"Yes, Drill Sergeant!"

"Don't get cute with me or I'll get the water hose."

I watched as she sped down the street and then made my way to the kitchen. Looking around the small area, the aroma of cookies danced like sugarplums through my mind. However, it was short lived when I opened the refrigerator. Ye, Gods, it was beginning to reek. This would be my first operative…get it cleaned. Grabbing up a box of heavy duty, lawn and leaf garbage bags, I popped one of the bags open filling its interior with smelly old condiments and moldy food. Several full bags later, I placed them outside by the street curb where the refuse department would see them for pick-up. A stiff spray of Lysol filled the whole house. One job down and ten thousand to go.

So many cooking utensils scattered across the linoleum made it difficult to create a path. In earnest, I selected a few of the better ones and tossed the rest. Garbage bags splitting at the seams made it complicated to carry them to the garage. *How in thunder could one little woman use all these pots and pans?*

Perhaps tossing them wasn't the answer. I decided to put them on the curb with a sign; "free for the taking". Surely to goodness, there was someone who could put them to use.

In the corner of the garage was my old red wagon. I had no idea Mom still had the contraption. Worn tires, bent shaft and scraped paint were the glue holding it together. It creaked as I moved it from its resting place and the metal peeking through worn tires scraped the pavement. You could almost hear the agony with its painful travel. Securing the pots and pans, I wheeled them to the curb. Saturday morning would have the faded red, cobblestone road heavy with traffic.

I watched from the corner of the garage. Sure enough, within seconds a young woman and her two little girls were gathering up the needed items. I felt warm inside, knowing the cookie sheets would be put to use. After they drove down the street, I retrieved my wagon; knowing it would be used many times today.

Melissa honked the horn; signaling me to help unload the banana boxes. "Did I see someone hauling stuff from the curb?"

"Sure enough, my lady. It's a good thing you came when you did or I might have given away the whole house. Oh, Melissa, you should have seen the excitement of those little girls. Their eyes were as big as saucers; screaming about a cookie sheet. I almost cried."

"Todd Jenkins, you're an old softie. Here, make yourself useful and carry these boxes inside. Wow, I'm impressed. You've done a great job in the kitchen."

"For a one legged man, I can do a fair heap of work. I nearly broke my neck when I stepped in one of those stupid canning contraptions. My prosthesis slid on a garbage bag and my good leg wound up inside it. I was sliding all over the place. If it hadn't been for the sink holding me up, I might have been a goner."

"I wish I had been here to capture the moment on camera."

"Will you stop laughing? You're making me laugh and I can't stand up when I get hysterical."

"But it sounds so funny. I promise not to tease you about it." Melissa walked to the front room, sat down and laughed again.

"I told you to stop laughing," Todd snickered. *She sure brightens up a room.* "Hey, Melissa, care to join me for a cup of instant coffee? I found a jar of amaretto in the cabinet. I've not tasted this brand but it sure smells good."

Melissa sauntered back to the kitchen and sniffed the delicacy. "One cup, you hear? There's still too much we need to get done around here." Melissa put the cup to her lips and sipped the delectable coffee. "Well, maybe two cups. This tastes yummy."

It was 11:00 a.m. when we sat down at the dinette and began talking. "Todd, I think if we take one room a day, the house will be cleaned out in no time. From the appearance of the living room, your Mom was a good housekeeper. All the closets are neat and I don't see too much clutter. The only thing you will need to do is decide what you want to keep. Is there anything special or some kind of treasure you particularly want to take home?"

"There are a few Hummel figures I want to enjoy. I gave those to Mom as Christmas presents. Of course, any pictures she has boxed away, I want those and personal records." Todd pondered over objects he had been surrounded by as a child and knew the one thing he wanted-- letters from his father. He grew somber.

"What's the problem, Todd? Did I say something to upset you?"

"No. I was thinking about Dad and the letters he sent to Mom. They are around here somewhere. I just want to be certain they weren't discarded. They were personal and I'm not sure I will ever read them but, at least I will have them. All of the letters I received from him were inside my Patch Dimple. Lost forever."

"Why on earth don't you put an advertisement in the newspaper and try to locate Patch Dimple? There has to be someone in this town who bought him. Maybe they would be willing to give him back to you."

"I don't think it would be possible. It was so many years ago."

"Well, if he was as ugly as you described, you can rest assured someone will remember it. If you don't try, you will never know."

"Let's change the subject, shall we? What about you, Melissa? I've told you all there is to know about me, now it's your turn."

"Hmmm…there's not much to tell. I'm divorced, no children, living with my mom…a nurse. Exciting, uh?"

"Oh, come off it. You told me about being a nurse but what about the ex husband?"

"He was a jerk. I met Ralph on a blind date. He said all the right things and was charming. He said all the sweet nothings a girl longs to hear. I wish I had ear plugs in my ears. Boy, talk about hindsight."

"How long were you married?"

"Three years too damned long. At first, he was as sweet as slow moving molasses but it was the side he wanted me to see. I was ignorant to what he was actually like. It took me about one year to fully gather my senses but it was too late. He had taken from me all the things which should have been cherished."

"What do you mean, taken from you?"

"Oh, I'm not talking about money. It's taken me a long time to get back my self respect. Actually, self respect is not a good description. It's more like suspicion. I didn't trust anyone. He was a thief, taking my trust and turning me into an empty shell. While I was working the night shift, he was working the system of ladies. I honestly thought we were a couple of love birds waiting to fill the nest. Boy, was I in for a rude slap in the face. One night while working in the emergency room, I fell over a cart. Someone had moved it in an area thinking it would be out of the way but it wasn't. When I stumbled into it, the whole thing upended making the wheel do an upper cut to my chin. It hit me so hard, I couldn't see straight; my ribs felt like they were crushed."

"What does it have to do with your divorce?"

"I'm getting there. They did an x-ray on my ribs but nothing was broken, so my superior, in her dedicated stance, decided the best place for me was at home. Since I couldn't see, I couldn't drive. I left my car at the hospital and one of my friends drove me home. When I unlocked the front door I didn't suspect a thing. The only thing I could think about was the excruciating headache and blurry eyes. When I staggered into the bedroom, Ralph was there with a group of men and women."

"Whoa! Don't go any further. You're getting into a detail I don't want to know. Skip this part and tell me why it took three years to divorce him. It doesn't make sense."

"Don't you understand? I am like any other woman who wants her marriage to succeed. A part of the vows; till death do us part was the way I was raised. The next full year, we went to counseling. He promised to be faithful and I thought it was working. Then out of the blue, I caught him slipping blue under-panties out of the trunk of the car. They weren't mine. I confronted him; he slapped me telling me I was the cause of his problems and then proceeded to beat the hell out of me."

"What did you do?"

"I pressed charges against him and filed for divorce. It was the best thing I ever did. When we went to court for his domestic violence, he tried to sway the female judge with his charm. She saw through his little charade, fined him a hefty sum and put him on probation. I filed an order of protection against him and went ahead with the divorce proceedings. He tried to coo me back, but I had him arrested for violating the protective order. Since no one would bail him out of jail, he stayed there till his hearing.

The court had a heyday with him…more fines. Then it came time for our divorce hearing. He tried to prove he was the one getting the raw deal but when they saw pictures of me, battered and bloody, I was granted the divorce. Six months later, I was free of him. It was final."

"How did the two of you manage to live in the same town? Weren't you scared?"

"He was more afraid of me than I of him. His friends got wise and didn't want to have anything to do with him and his small business all but dried up. Paranoia was at an all time high with him. Besides, he was a Vietnam War Veteran and to tell you the truth, he had more problems than hopping in the sack with women. He still hasn't gotten the help he needs. Last word I heard, he was moving to Arizona. What more do you want to know?"

"What brought you back to this area?"

Melissa looked at me. "I'll have to show you." Bending over to lift her sweat pants leg she pointed. "This is why I came back. I had a major varicose vein burst in my leg. It started out as a regular varicose vein; bulging from pressure. Walking the concrete halls in the hospital didn't help. My leg began to swell and the doctor told me it was possible I had a deep vein thrombosis. When the doctor stripped my vein, I was relieved to know it was just expanded but it continued to throb. It's a wonder I didn't die; you know blood clots. I took a leave of absence from work, came home to see Mom and decided not to go back."

I glared at Melissa. "Then why in the world did you say you would help me with all this work? You should be home with your leg propped up."

"Fiddle faddle! I can't stay propped up forever. The doctors told me to take caution and I am not about to do anything to make it worse. I have it wrapped with an ACE bandage and as long as I know my limitations I will be fine. Look at the clock, Todd. We have been talking for two hours. We need to get a move on. Get out of your chair, put the lid on the coffee and let's get to work."

We completed the kitchen, moving on to the small bathroom but all the while, I kept hearing Melissa's words about putting an ad in the paper to find Patch Dimple. Opening the drawers to the vanity, thoughts of Patch Dimple dissipated as Mom's personal hygiene products leaped at me. Asking Melissa if she would discard the unmentionables; she laughed exclaiming it only contained products all women need. I left Melissa to do the dirty work telling her she could have anything she wished. Mom's perfumes captured

Melissa as she sniffed each of the scents. While she pursued the remaining items cowering in the linen closet, I cleaned out the hall closet.

In no time we managed to toss several years of accumulation in the trash bin. Bath towels and linens would be donated, old toys from the hall closet would be put in a garage sale and her work coats and clothing would be cleaned and given to a charity. The only rooms left to be cleaned were the bedrooms, living area, garage and attic. It would be a task to remember.

It was time to call it a day since other things beckoned. Patches would be frothing at the mouth to get out of the house and anxious to eat when her foray was completed. I knew Melissa must be tired. Although she didn't complain, I didn't want to keep her on her legs any longer than necessary. Even though I was tired, cleaning the house rejuvenated my spirits and propelled me to clean my own home. Melissa and I drove to the Sonic, picked up our favorite fast meal and sped toward the house. En route, both of us were hungry and sniggered as we lurched for the fries, giggling as they spilled on the floorboard.

We pulled into the driveway and I noticed my mailbox lying on the ground. Mail was strewn all over the small lawn. I told Melissa to let Patches come outside with me as I'd be inside as soon as I unearthed the mystery of the mail caper. I retrieved the letters and hoped no important mail had been lost or blown into another yard. The mail carrier had penned a note: "You need to replace or repair this mail box. The wood post will not continue to hold the tin box. Future delivery will be terminated until this has been completed. Your mail will be held at the post office. Hours are from 9:00 a.m. until 5:00 p.m."

Well, now it appears I have put off doing things around this place. Mom, you've made me sit up and take notice of my surroundings. Things must get done and I promise this will be on my agenda.

Patches loped across the lawn, greeting me with her lanky body and feet the size of small melons. She was a vision of beauty with her face laced with a patch across one eye and a white spot for a dimple. Jumping up to greet me, it was like an old friend coming home from a war. For a few minutes, we wrestled upon the ground like two little kids fumbling for a greased football. She knew she was queen of the manor and proved it on more than one occasion. I couldn't win; I melted like putty when Patches stared at me.

Melissa yelled, "Are you two going to stay out there the rest of the day? Food's getting cold."

"Oops, Patches, another female is yelling. We'd better go inside before she comes out here with a broom." Patches stared at me with her soulful eyes. Food!

"What's up with the mail box?"

"Oh, the stupid post has rotted out and if I don't get it fixed, they won't deliver my mail. I'm famished. Let's eat."

I started to pour Patches her meal but realized Melissa had already done the job. "Patches, you'd better thank Melissa. Go give her a sloppy kiss."

Melissa held up her hand. "Don't you dare, Patches! Right now I don't want to fight you for my burger. My teeth are the only ones taking a bite from it."

The atmosphere was splendid and I couldn't help but wonder how my life might have been if I had remarried. I loved having Melissa with me but knew it might not be in the picture for us to be together. Maybe I thought it could happen but for now I would have to settle on being work mates. She would go home tonight; I would be here. Time would tell, but for now we didn't need to make conversation; being together was perfect.

Six

The next week was tedious. Melissa phoned to tell me she couldn't help me finish cleaning Mom's house. Not being one to pry, I told her I understood even though I didn't. We had such a great time; laughing and enjoying each other's company. Instead of feeling sorry for myself, I spent my time clearing out my garage and repairing the mail box.

Surprisingly, I was able to do a lot of things in a short time. I piled items needing to go to the dump in the back of my car and disposed of it in a hurry. No need to hang onto junk or look at it each time I passed through the garage. Now my car had a place of its' own. Patches and I were accustomed to being by ourselves and it actually wasn't so bad.

On Friday, Patches and I had to go to the vet. Her rabies shot was necessary and so were city tags. On our way, we stopped at the local pet store to purchase a long leash. The leash I had was too small for her neck so I cut up a belt to accommodate the slack needed. Since dogs were allowed inside the pet store, Patches and I moseyed inside.

She was exuberant with antagonizing aromas of dog treats and she was in awe of the other animals. She had never been close to another dog or even seen a cat. She sniffed a ferret's cage and then jumped when the ferret lunged toward her and barked as hamsters engaged squeaking wheels. It was a new world for her. Choosing a leash, we made our way to the checkout counter. On an end cap, next to the register, were various stuffed animals. One in particular caught my attention and immediately transfixed me in a trance.

The fluffy teddy bear was the same color of my Patch Dimple or partially, that is, until material slowly took the place of its original form. I couldn't stand thinking of it anymore so I put a plan of action in the back of my mind. I would try to locate Patch Dimple.

I paid for the leash and as usual, Patches was the center of attention. The sales lady commented on Patches, a comment making me think of Melissa. It was the second time someone said Patches looked familiar; first Melissa and now the sales lady. Perhaps I should have placed an article in the lost and found section of the newspaper when I found Patches. It never crossed my mind since other things were at the forefront of my existence. Placing my wallet in my trouser pocket, I thanked her and we left.

Anxious to get out of the store before someone yelled, "That's my dog!" we hastily made our way to the car. There was no way in hell anyone would get this dog back. I didn't care if the world turned green with envy, Patches was my dog and no one would get her. Lucky for us, no one at the vet store or on the parking lot made any such comment.

We were just about a half block from home when I saw Melissa backing out of my driveway. Honking my horn to get her to stop was fruitless. I sped up as fast as I could but she turned the corner without looking back. I was crushed but turned my car around and went home.

There was a note taped to the garage door: *Todd, sorry to have missed you. Call me when you get home.* Patches and I raced inside. She thought I wanted to play and was unhappy when I didn't return the signal. She lay down on her bed and I went to the phone.

"Hello?"

"This is Todd Jenkins. Is Melissa there?"

"I'm afraid not. She went out and hasn't returned."

"I see. Will you tell her Todd Jenkins phoned?"

"Sure. Oh, wait a minute; she just came in the door."

I could hear her say, "Who is it, Mom? It's not Ralph, is it?" Her mom must have shaken her head because I didn't hear her reply. Several minutes later, Melissa came to the phone.

"Hi, Todd, I see you found my note. How are you doing?"

"I am doing fine. We've missed seeing you. Didn't you hear me honking my horn at you? Patches and I tried to catch up to you but weren't able. Sorry we weren't here when you came by."

"How is the house cleaning coming along?"

"I haven't gone back over there but I did manage to clean my own house and fix the mail box. Melissa, I want to know something. Did I say or do anything to make you uneasy? I mean, while we were at Mom's house?"

"No, why do you ask?"

"You were so abrupt about not wanting to help me and I just thought I did something wrong."

"It's not you, Todd. It's Ralph."

"What about Ralph? I thought you said he was in Arizona."

"Not any more. He's here in town and not a happy camper. I was afraid to leave my mother alone in the house."

"He wouldn't do anything to your mother, would he?"

"I don't know what he is liable to do. He phoned me wanting to get back together."

"I thought you had a protective order against him."

"Yeah, I do but it's for another state. I had to go to the police station this morning and enact another order. They can't do anything until he makes a move."

"I'm sorry you have to go through this ordeal."

"So am I but it's the price I have to pay having been married to the nut. Sometimes, Todd, I wish I could flail the bastard with a whip, and inflict on him the type of pain I endured from his constant barrage of mental and physical abuse. He's one mean son-of-a-bitch and I hate his guts. If he so much as comes within one hundred feet of me, I am liable to kill him, so, I am hoping, with this new order of protection, he will understand I mean business."

"Why does he continue to hound you?"

"He's afraid of being left alone. It has something to do with Vietnam."

"If he is our age, he wouldn't have been in Vietnam."

"He is sixteen years older. Don't even make a remark about me marrying someone older. I have heard it all before and reminders make me shiver. We can talk about it later, when we go to your mom's house."

"When we go to Mom's house? Is it why you came by my house? To tell me you've changed your mind?"

"Yes, I wanted to let you know I have decided to help you. It is time for me to take a stand against Ralph and be my own person. I am tired of looking over my shoulder wondering where he will pop up. When would you like to go to your mom's?"

"How about right now? Unless you have other things to do, I can pick you up. There's something I would like to tell you but it will wait."

"Now will be fine but give me a few minutes so I can change my clothes. How about sandwiches? I can throw together some tuna. You bring the drinks."

"Sounds great, Melissa. We'll see you in about twenty minutes."

I was elated Melissa changed her mind. I quickly put

some cola's in a cooler, slung some potato chips in a sack and jerked up Patches leash. "Patches, do you want to go, girl? You've never been to Mom's house. You'll have to stay inside cause there is no fenced area. Well, are you going to bark or sit there looking at me?" Patches let out a few half hearted woofs and headed for the door. "Wait a minute, Patches. Don't get in such a hurry. We need your food, too." I picked up her sack of chow, put the leash on her collar and headed toward the car.

"Patches, stay in the back seat. Melissa has to sit up front with me. I've got to put this stuff in the trunk or you'll be all over it. Stay, girl." Getting Patches to stay in the back seat would be a miracle. She was used to sitting in the front with her head hanging out the window. I lifted the trunk of my car and stopped. It had been awhile since I had the need to use the trunk and forgot about articles left there.

Mom's purse was glaring me as if I had deliberately forgotten about it. It had taken on a persona of its own, encouraging me to retrieve it from its tomb. My hands shook, knowing I would be holding my mom once again, in my arms.

It was ridiculous. It was just a purse and wasn't going to bite me. I hadn't even looked inside it since she died. I don't know why I was so afraid of a little purse.

The trunk closed with a thud, the purse still sleeping with its secret inside. I felt like a stupid coward. But it wasn't cowardice, not really. It belonged to Mom, not me. I was taught never to pry into someone's space. I sighed when I got into the car. "Melissa, you'll have the honors."

Patches looked forlorn as she crouched in the back seat. Now and then her head would pop over the seat with her legs trying in vain to maneuver into a front seat position. As we neared Melissa's house, she anxiously wagged her tail knowing her friend would be scratching her ears. She went ballistic as Melissa opened the car door, not so much for

Melissa but the food inside the sack she was carrying. I motioned for her to go to the trunk.

My face brightened as I greeted her. "Hello, Fair Lady, it sure is good to see you. You're a sight for sore eyes."

"You're not so bad yourself, kind Sir. What did you bring to eat? One sack is bulging," she said placing the tuna sandwiches inside a box.

"Just some dog food and drinks."

"It sure doesn't look like dog food to me. How many bags of potato chips did you bring? What else do you have shoved inside those sacks? Let me see."

"Oh, just a little barbecue ribs, sour cream and chive potato chips, some dips, cookies and dog food. Can't forget Patches, she'd woof down what we were trying to eat."

Melissa put her hands on her hips and chided. "Todd, do you carry a purse?"

"Certainly not. It's Mom's. I put it in the trunk and forgot all about it when the police gave it to me. I want you to go through its' contents, if you don't mind."

"Why on earth haven't you done it yourself?"

"I don't know. Somewhere in the back of my mind, I can still hear her telling me not to nose around in other people's property. Here, go through it while we drive. If there is anything in there I shouldn't know about, don't tell me."

"Todd, you are weird."

Out of the corner of my eye, I watched Melissa go through each compartment of the purse. I was curious but still apprehensive to know what kind of secrets she had. We were about two blocks from the house when Melissa let out a whoop.

"Oh, my God! Todd, you will never believe this. Pull over and look."

Whatever made Melissa go nuts scared the hell out

of me. I quickly turned into a parking lot. "What is it, Melissa?"

"I told you, I told you! Remember when I told you Patches looked familiar. Look at this receipt."

My hands were shaking so hard from Melissa's outburst, I wasn't sure I could read it. I blurted, "It's dated the day she died." The blood drained from my face as I read the description aloud. "Sold to: Thelma Jenkins: Pure bred German shepherd dog: Age; 12 weeks old: Sex; female: Total paid; $350.00."

Melissa patted me on the arm. "Todd, are you ok?"

"Not really. Patches was inside Mom's car the night she died. If I hadn't gone to the spot where she died, I would never have found Patches...she would have died too. She must have crawled out of the car window. No wonder her little paws were cut. Melissa, Patches was meant to be my Christmas present. Mom and I always bought each other a special present."

I turned to look at Patches and hugged her neck. "Patches, you were meant for me. Mom was rushing from working on the Christmas Bazaar items to buy you."

"Todd, there's another receipt. Wait a minute...it's a gift certificate for one year's supply of dog food. My Lord, Todd, there is five hundred dollars in here with a note attached: Use for chain link fence."

"Mom complained to me about my fence. She told me to get it fixed. I bet she was going to use the money to make sure it was repaired for my Patches. Mom was one of a kind. She knew I could afford to do things, but knew I liked to put things off, too. I will have to do as she wished and get the fence fixed. What else did she have hidden inside her purse?"

"There is a key to a safe deposit box and several pictures of you with some kind of weird looking critter. What is this thing, Todd?"

I didn't know what kind of critter it could be since we only had dogs. "It's Patch Dimple!"

"It is the ugliest thing I ever saw. What on earth is on its face?"

"Pieces of left over material Dad used to patch holes in its head. Dad never threw out scraps of material because he knew I would be yelling for him to sew up holes. The black material over his eye is like a pirate's eyepiece. I made the dimple. A long thread was hanging on the back of his head. When I pulled it tight, a dimple was created."

"Was Patch Dimple always like this?"

"No. He started off as a furry teddy bear but wound up looking like he had been in a cat fight. Most of the fur was chewed off by Dolly, our Dachshund. I sneaked up behind Dolly with my teddy bear pretending I was holding another dog. Before I knew what was happening, Dolly attacked it ripping it into pieces. My beloved Patch Dimple was born."

After the initial shock of having Melissa tell me the contents in the purse, we continued to the house. En route, I told Melissa about plans to hunt for Patch Dimple and she agreed to help me. This day was turning out to be an award winning event but unfortunately, we weren't prepared for what came next. A car was in the driveway.

"Don't stop, Todd. It's Ralph."

"He has no business being there. I damned well will stop and find out what he wants." I pulled in behind his car preventing him from leaving. I told Melissa to stay in the car and if she had to, phone the police on my cell phone. "What are you doing here? This is a private residence."

Ralph was leaning on his car door with his back to me. When he turned to face me, he appeared to be in a daze. Massive amounts of saliva ran out of the right side of his mouth and his right eye was drooping. When he spoke, it was apparent he was hurting. His words were slurred as he tried to tell me he needed to speak with Melissa. To tell you the truth, he scared me but I didn't want him to sense my fear.

Melissa wouldn't stay in the car and approached the two of us. "What do you want, Ralph? I am sick and tired of having you around me. You are not part of my life anymore. Can't you understand it?"

Ralph turned to face Melissa. He tried to explain to her that he only wanted to know what had happened to him. He was embarrassed to let anyone see him, especially a stranger. Knowing she was a nurse, she would be able to tell him what to do. "Melissa," Ralph's words were barely audible as he tried to form the consonants with his lips. "What's wrong with me?"

"You know I am not a doctor and won't give out unsubstantiated advice but by your facial expressions, you could have Bells Palsy. Why don't you go to the veteran's hospital and get proper medical advice?"

I was beginning to understand why Ralph needed to see Melissa and suggested we go inside the house to talk. We didn't need the neighbors thinking we were having a brawl. Ralph was hesitant but relented. Melissa was angry for the interruption. Patches was indifferent and I was anxious because all I wanted to do was clean out the house. It was one damned thing after another. The house had been put on hold again.

Ralph apologized for approaching the two of us. It was more than I could stand to see this man whimpering. The visual aspect was even more discouraging knowing whatever struck him could strike anyone. The distortion of his face created muscle weakness leaving his lower jaw gaping open. He couldn't completely close his mouth. Saliva oozed and dripped down the crease of his sagging lips. When he tried to close his eyes, one of them stayed open. He complained of excruciating pain behind his ears, like sharp daggers piercing and gouging bone.

I was at a loss for words and excused myself. Patches and I unloaded the trunk of the car and went to the kitchen. Conversation between Ralph and Melissa was becoming loud, too loud for my liking. Then all of a sudden, it was quiet. Patches and I gingerly tiptoed to the living room.

Ralph was lying on the couch and Melissa was on the phone. I wasn't sure if she had knocked him in the head or to whom she was talking. I was becoming uneasy. A one sided conversation became evident. "Yes, he's resting. When might he be able to see the doctor? I understand. He's a Vietnam veteran. I am not sure where his medical records are, but I believe, they used to be on file at the Veteran's Hospital in Jackson. Yes, Ma'am, I'll be certain he is there tomorrow at 8:00 a.m."

"Talking to the doctor?" I quizzed Melissa.

"No, it was the receptionist. She made an appointment for Ralph to see the doctor. Todd, he probably has Bells Palsy. It's not a lasting affliction but can scare a body to death. He doesn't appear to have blisters inside his mouth, indicating another mimicking disease."

I shrugged. "Should he be driving? Man, he spooked me!"

"The only thing he needs to do is cover his affected eye to keep it from drying out. I guess I will have to drive him home, Todd, and take him to the doctor tomorrow morning. Damn! I've tried to get away from him and he keeps coming back like a boomerang. Just once I wish the boomerang would hit something, like it's supposed to do and not come back to me."

"Why don't you just leave him on the couch? He's not hurting anything. I don't suspect he is too eager to do a footrace. He sure doesn't look like he could do too much harm. Just let him sleep."

"Sounds good to me. I am worn out from doing nothing. It will be a welcomed change to get to work. Where do you want to start?"

"Why don't we go up to the attic? We'll start at the top and work down. I've already taken some boxes up there. We don't have to sweep. When the house is cleaned out, I will have a cleaning crew do the details."

Walking into the hallway, I pulled on the old rope hanging from the ceiling. Unfolding the hinged ladder, it exposed narrow steep rungs. "Do you want me to go first or will you?"

"Are you sure this thing is safe? You'd better go first and let me watch you fall. I'd rather it be you than me."

"It's safe. It's a mite shaky but it will hold our weight. Come on but be careful of the hinges. Don't hit your legs on it."

"How in the world did anyone get stuff up here?"

"Usually, I would go upstairs and Mom would lift boxes up to me. This pull down ladder wasn't always here. You should have seen what the opening looked like before I installed this access. It was nothing more than a hole in the ceiling, covered with a piece of sheetrock. You had to use an expandable ladder to get up there. It was no picnic."

"It doesn't look like a picnic to me right now either."

"This is a piece of cake without the picnic, Melissa. When I was small, Dad used it for his sewing area. I don't remember in detail, but he would dissemble pieces of large equipment and take it up, section by section. You are going to be surprised; it's larger up here than it appears."

We scaled the ladder while Patches watched. I didn't try to coax Patches up the stairs because her gangly legs would have slipped between the rungs. If she had started to howl, Ralph might have gone off the deep end. Melissa reminded me sharp noises increase pain to those having Bells Palsy. We tried to keep the noise to a minimum. I flicked on the light switch.

"Good grief, Todd, what is all this stuff. I thought you said your mom had a garage sale and got rid of things."

"She did. This is bits and pieces left over from a lifetime."

"You can say that again! What is this dreadful thing? It looks as though it could devour an elephant."

"It's Dad's old sewing machine. Don't ask me how it works. I would sit up here watching him thread it but never remembered how he did it. Do you sew, Melissa?"

"Yeah, I know how to sew but I learned on a Treadle Machine. This thing could knit a whole afghan, throw it on the bed and cover you up. It's spooky. What is this pile of stuff? Ooh, something moved. I don't like it up here."

"Material, patterns, chalk and his sewing basket is in this pile." I reached over to uncover the ominous moving creature. "This is a dress form."

"It's just like something from a scary movie. Move it under the light. It's eerie knowing it's staring at me from a dark corner."

I sat down and laughed. "It doesn't have a head on it."

"I don't care, throw it down the stairs! Do something with it."

"I'd better not throw it down the stairs because Patches would come unglued. There's no telling what Ralph would do. He's liable to shoot up the house. Melissa, he doesn't have a gun on him, does he?"

"Why'd you ask such a stupid question? I don't know. He used to carry a gun because he thought the enemy was after him. He was paranoid."

"Don't be telling me crap like that. Mom used to tell me an ax murderer would sneak up on me one day and chop me to bits. Geesh, Melissa, I guess I could take off my leg and whack him in the head but then how would I run?"

"Well, I sure as hell am not going to carry you. Todd Jenkins, you are the funniest man I have ever known. It feels good to laugh." Melissa reached over and hugged me. "You know something? Since I have been with you, I have laughed more than I ever thought possible."

I was ready to kiss Melissa but was interrupted with the sound of the front door slamming. Peeking out the dormer window, I viewed Ralph driving across the front lawn. "Melissa, Ralph has gone nuts. He is tearing up the lawn! Stay up here and I will go see what the problem is."

"Just be careful, Todd. There is no way to predict what he will do."

Scrambling down the ladder, I ran to the front door. Standing on the front porch, I screamed for Ralph. Ralph ignored me and continued to upend shrubs and flowers. Without warning, Ralph drove straight in my direction. The one finger salute hailed through the open window of the car and slurred profanities echoed in the air.

"Stop, Ralph, before you kill yourself. Turn off the motor, or I'll call the police." Ralph slammed on the brakes within inches of where I was standing on the porch.

"What the hell is the matter with you, Ralph? Are you always as obnoxious as you appear?"

"Don't give me the song and dance routine." Ralph slobbered, trying to intimidate me. "What makes you think you are better than I am? You don't know anything about me but you go around with your nose stuck up in the air."

"What are you rambling? No, I don't know you personally and to tell the truth, I don't want to know you. You are a first class jerk. What is stuck in your craw?"

"You and this whole country are stuck in my craw. I've been through hell and no one gives a damned whether I live or die."

"Control yourself, Ralph. You have more problems than I can manage and you need professional help. Why don't you stop and think. I have had no personal dealings with you to make you go in such a rage."

Ralph glared at me with blood in his eyes. "The whole damned country has screwed me over and you are no exception."

"You make no sense whatsoever. Get out of the car, Ralph, before we both wind up in jail. The neighbors don't take kindly to this type of exhibition. One of them will surely phone the police."

"I don't care if they phone the National Guard or send out snipers. Maybe one of them would end my misery. It's hell on this planet."

"I've had enough of your insanity and so has Melissa. Have you ever stopped to think what kind of hell and torture she has been through because of your idiocy? She didn't ask for your off the wall tirades, but you managed to sling your inability to cope with life on her."

"You don't have a clue about life. Don't stand there with your holier than thou attitude and tell me I don't know about life. I've seen more mayhem, death and torture than you will have seen in ten life times. I and other men have been put through the ringer for your rotten ass and all the other screwed up minds for the last thirty some odd years."

"Why don't we talk about it? Instead of you sitting in the car like some wild maniac, come back in the house and fill me in. I'm game to listen to your ravings, but I will not subject Melissa to any more of your insane actions. If you want to talk, come inside; otherwise, get the hell off this property."

Neighbors were beginning to gather in driveways watching the two of us rant and rave. I could tell they were becoming panicked with the thought of some lunatic going off the deep end and shooting people for the fun of it. I didn't want to admit my fear but fear was primary in my mind. It was the first time in my life to see someone be adamant about death and not care if blood and guts were smeared all over the pavement.

I thought about The Twin Towers and how those persons must have felt, knowing a terrorist was at the helm of an airplane, directing it toward the massive buildings. Many things surged through my mind and I wondered if terrorists had the kind of rage that exploded inside Ralph's mind. I extended my hand. "Come on, Ralph, let's go inside and talk man to man about what's eating you."

I thought Ralph would take my suggestion to heart and do as I wished, but he didn't. He started the motor of the car, slammed it into reverse digging up grass and dirt like a back hoe. He was on a mission of destruction and didn't care who was hurt. When he put the car in drive to exit the yard, police had arrived on the scene. Squad cars were in plain view with patrolmen trying to get him to talk. With each rev of the engine, we knew something was going to happen but didn't know what to expect. Melissa had joined me on the front porch to get Ralph calmed down. Seeing her stand by me was like someone pouring salt into a gaping wound. It was the straw to break the camel's back.

Ralph, the ticking time bomb with threats of detonation, and eyes darting with fury, slowly turned off the motor, slumping over the steering wheel.

Melissa was frantic. "All of you, back off." They obliged her wishes and she approached Ralph. "Just what do you think you were doing? You aren't stupid, Ralph. There is help for you if you would only allow it to happen. Why don't you let me set up an appointment at the Veteran's Hospital?"

"I've been there before, Melissa. All the doctors tell me it's not real. I'm only putting myself through self destruction because there is no medical explanation for my condition. I've told them how I feel. It's real, Melissa, it's real. It's not a fabrication. My mind replays every mission I was on in 'Nam. I can't shut out the blood, the arms and legs blown to bits or the bombs exploding around me. What in God's name am I supposed to do? Tell me, Melissa—tell me! You're the only one who can help me."

"No, I am not, Ralph. I thought I understood you when I married you, but I didn't. Your problem is deeper than anything I might say or do. I am not qualified to give mental evaluations. All I know is I was subjected to your abuse, infidelities, and rage. If you don't get some help, you may never come to grips with your emotions. Those who have loved you have been tormented with your unwillingness to get help."

"I've tried, Melissa. The doctors push me aside as though I have the plague. I haven't been given my full disability because papers have been lost or destroyed. It's like I don't exist, like I was never in Vietnam…never experienced what I did. I've been shoved aside ever since I got back from Vietnam. What am I supposed to do?"

"I don't have the answer to your question but I am willing to go with you to find someone who can. The promise I will make is I will be your friend as long as you treat me with respect. If you don't get help, don't come around me again. It's your decision."

Ralph sat in his car, head drooped toward his chest. He pounded the steering wheel with his fists then quietly exited the car. Police officers rushed the car and handcuffed him. The situation had been defused. I was asked if I wished to press charges for damages done to the yard, but listening to Ralph begging Melissa for help made it hard for me to consider charges.

His outburst was a type of terrorist threat; rage, trespassing and personal property damage. Clearly Ralph needed help and to inflict jail time on him would not get the job done. I declined and hoped my decision would not be a bad one. The unfortunate thing was, Ralph was handcuffed and placed inside the patrol car. Not because of his disruptive behavior but because he tried to hit a police officer and lunged for the pistol strapped to the officers waist. I could hear Ralph screaming, "Won't someone kill me and put me out of my misery? Blow my head off and stop the torture raging inside me!"

Seeing the exposure of Ralph's mindset, many things raced across the screen of my memory. The thought of Dad in Vietnam and the conversation Mom and I had, hit me in the face. Dad could have been the same way. The horror of Vietnam or any war must be so harrowing the soldiers can't erase or put aside the viciousness sheathed in their mind's eye. Somehow I would find an avenue to understand Vietnam.

Melissa and I returned to the house. The scale of what we had witnessed put a damper on our enthusiastic finds in the attic. Even the hug Melissa gave me seemed superficial, compared to the problems Ralph had deep within his soul. We were quiet as we went about the duty set before us. The mannequin dress form lost the luster in laughter and paled as we half heartedly went about our routine. It cast a dark shadow and left the two of us in a murky gap. The turmoil inside my stomach left a bad taste in my mouth.

Melissa broke my thoughts. "Todd, I am so sorry you were subjected to Ralph. Had I known he would react so violently, I would not have come here today."

"It's not your fault, Melissa. You didn't know this would happen."

"Maybe I did…not at this exact time but I knew he would eventually lose it. It's been trying to surface for a long time. Red flags were there, every time he felt the paranoia close him into a shell. He would be passive for awhile and all of a sudden explode like a stick of dynamite. I recognized the symptoms of edging insanity but he never would talk about what he saw in Vietnam."

"How old was he when he left for Vietnam?"

"He was eighteen and just out of high school. All his buddies were drafted at the same time. Some of them only returned in body bags. He and his best friend were shipped out the same day but soon lost sight of each other. Ralph went one way and Sonny went the other. Sonny died in a helicopter crash and Ralph never got over it."

"Did he say anything about Vietnam?"

"A few words. I remember Ralph having nightmares, lashing out to ghosts around him. He destroyed a pillow with his fists one night and didn't remember it the next day. He accused me of trying to make him crazy. I was always the brunt of his rage. I still have the scars to prove it."

"Isn't there anyone who can help him? Surely he has seen doctors."

"Ralph has been to more doctors in one day than I will ever see in a life time. His first full week of being home is when the visions returned. He had them in Vietnam but you don't just see a doctor when you feel the urge to phone one up. He told me his first visit with a doctor was less than he expected. The doctor told him nothing was wrong with him and gave him a handful of medications to take for headaches. All it did was create more problems. The second doctor told him to grow up, stop being a cry baby and get on with his life. From then on, it has been down hill all the way."

"His problems couldn't be any worse than other veterans. There are other soldiers going through the same problems, aren't there?"

"Thousands of them have the same symptoms. Some men would come to the hospital with hands so shaky they couldn't hold a glass of water. Unless there is a definable medical term, a doctor can't honestly diagnose a condition. What all these men need is a doctor who served in Vietnam. One who has seen and experienced the same day in and day out confrontations."

"I guess Mom was right. Until the government recognizes the veteran's plight, they will continue to suffer through endless hours of guilt, pain and persecution."

"Hey, Todd, I am tired of talking about something I can't change. I am hungry, how about you?"

"Yes, I am and I bet Patches has raided her sack full of food. Let's go eat. While we are filling our mouths, let's write out an ad for the paper. Maybe I will get a response from someone who has Patch Dimple. Who knows, he could be right here in the neighborhood. I promise not to ask any more questions about Ralph. Pact?"

"Pact."

Seven

Several days passed before I heard another word about Ralph. Melissa and I had managed to clear out most of the house to get it ready to put on the market. Twinges of guilt grew inside me because putting Mom's house on the market was something I really didn't want to do. I was aware that owning two houses was more than I could manage but a nagging temptation gnawed with my feelings. Maybe it was because it was the only thing I had left of my childhood and an apron string I wasn't ready to cut. Perhaps there was another reason, something I didn't know existed.

I was about to leave for town when Melissa phoned me. She was at the hospital and needed reassurance. By the tone of her voice, I knew it was serious. She told me she would fill me in when I got there. Although I had no desire to sit in a waiting room, I needed to be there for her. Our relationship had not grown in the way I desired but I grew to accept it. She was a friend, a good friend and I wouldn't let her down.

The parking lot was filled to capacity. It was hard to believe so many persons could be ill at the same time, but we're human and humans do fall prey to many diseases. I thought how lucky I was to have gotten a flu shot.

After driving around in circles, crisscrossing each section of parking isles, I found a spot large enough to squeeze in my car. The cars on either side were close and I had to wiggle to try and remove myself from the driver's seat. At one point I actually thought I would have to take off my prosthesis to get out of my car. It just didn't want to budge.

Lucky for me, the owner of the car to my driver's side told me to wait, he would back out. I was relieved to know I wouldn't have to undo my trousers to take off my leg. I breathed a sigh of relief but chastised myself for being so stupid for parking where I shouldn't. Sometimes I forget about my leg and think that I am more able bodied than I really am.

I made my way inside the hospital to the sixth floor. Stepping off the elevator, my stomach cringed. The hallway was clearly lit but the sounds permeating the floor echoed with a thunderous roar. Each consecutive ward had a heavy door with a small window. I have to admit, it frightened me not knowing what I was going to see or hear.

The nurses sat at the front desk, directly in front of the elevator. They must have had nerves made of steel to listen to the moans, screams and threats. I wanted to turn and run but knew Melissa needed me. Melissa was sitting in the small waiting room. Her smile brightened and soothed my fears. I asked what this floor was called. She replied, "Psychiatric wards."

Melissa took me by the hand and explained why she needed me. "Ralph tried to commit suicide."

"How did it happen?"

"When the police took him to jail, he couldn't make bond. When I got home the day he went nuts in your front yard, there was a message on my recorder begging me to pay his fines and put up bail. When I phoned the police station, they let me talk to Ralph. I refused his request, telling him he needed to get help. He began screaming profanities and told me the next time I saw him, he would be in a coffin. I found out he attacked an officer with the telephone receiver as he was hanging up the phone."

"Well, how did he get here? I thought he had agreed to go to the Veteran's Hospital. Isn't that where he should be?"

"He should be in a Veteran's Hospital but this is how and why he's here. After our conversation, they led him to the jail cell. He had been strip searched before the call. While he was talking to my recorder, the police did not know he had picked up the bottom portion of a ball point pen. Apparently it was inside the telephone cord...the kind of cord that looks like a coil. He hid it in his mouth."

"What happened next?"

"From what I understand, he was in a cell with two other men. When they called lights out, the two men laid down on the mattresses provided. He curled up on the floor mumbling it's where he belonged...in the gutter with the vermin. Besides, the other men weren't too happy the way Ralph's face sagged and told him to keep his distance."

"He was supposed to see a doctor about Bells Palsy, wasn't he?"

"He didn't make it. The police agreed to escort him to the doctor's office and I was to meet them there but..."

"Don't cry, Melissa. You've done all the right things for him and you're still by his side."

"Todd, I don't love him like I did when we were married. Things changed a long time ago. I see him now as a disturbed man who has caught up with himself."

"What did he do to be confined here?"

"Like I said, lights were out and the two men were asleep. Ralph took the ball point pen and rammed it into his stomach. He did it several times. When one of the men woke up to use the toilet, the lights from a street lamp showed blood smeared on the wall above the toilet. The man began screaming and the police rushed Ralph to the hospital."

"Shouldn't he be in a regular room?"

"Not after what he did. I just found out, Ralph has been here in the hospital for a week. When he recovered from the puncture wounds and they started to release him back to the police, he began to scream, rant and rave...to find me. They shuffled him up here until the Veteran's Hospital could be contacted."

"Has he done anything else, attacked anyone?"

"Yes. When he told the police worms were crawling all over him, he lunged for the police officer and hit him in the mouth. He also told them the black wall was waiting for his name."

"Black wall...what is a black wall?"

"He doesn't make any sense, Todd. He is quiet for awhile and then his eyes roll to the back of his head. It's as though he is trying to see the back of his brain."

"Have you tried to talk to him, reason with him?"

"Just one time, Todd. He began telling me eyes were following him and then he dug his fingernails into his flesh. I asked what he was doing and he told me, "Writing my name."

"Do you have any idea what he was trying to say?"

Melissa stared out the narrow waiting room window, her face grew solemn. "Todd, what am I going to do? Ralph and I are divorced. There is no legal thing I can do. I can't just waltz into a doctor's office and demand Ralph be declared mentally incompetent. A judge would laugh in my face. There is no love; no binding marital status, what should I do next?"

"I don't have a clue. Doesn't he have any money left from the company his dad left him? What about family, could they declare him unstable?"

"He went bankrupt when I divorced him. He went through tons of money and I don't know how he spent it. All I know is it wasn't spent on me. I didn't get a dime when we divorced. Money didn't mean a thing to me. All I wanted was a happy marriage, children..."

"You've never said much about his extended family. Could they help?"

"His mother passed away before his father did. Ralph does have a sister but they aren't close. When Ralph came back from 'Nam, he tried to live with her until he got established. One evening he went berserk, tearing up everything in sight. She kicked him out and told him never to contact her. I don't even know where she lives."

"Didn't you ever talk to her?"

"Are you kidding? One time when I told Ralph we should phone her to tell her we were married, he jerked the phone out of the wall. He made me promise never to mention her name again. I never brought up the subject again. I have never spoken to her and wouldn't know her if I met her on the street."

"Well, something needs to be done. Do you think he would talk to me?"

"He might but there is no guarantee. The way he is right now, you might not want to see him."

"Why?"

"He is strapped down."

"Strapped down? Is he as volatile as you make it sound?"

"Yes. They had to sedate him just to get him on the bed. If you think you could talk to him, I will see if the nurses will allow you to enter his room."

"I'll give it a try."

Melissa and I went to the nurse's station and explained the situation. The nurses absolutely refused entry into Ralph's room until the doctor in charge could be contacted. They would not take responsibility for me entering the room. They told us to have a seat or go to the cafeteria while the doctor was paged. It would be awhile before they knew the results. I asked how we would know if the doctor agreed and was told our names would be announced on the intercom.

We were stepping out of the elevator at the cafeteria level when we heard the announcement for us to return to the sixth floor. In unison we blurted, "Well, that didn't take long." Back up the elevator we went.

Stepping from the elevator, Melissa grabbed my hand. Her hand was cold and she was shaking from head to toe. "Are you cold, Melissa?"

"No. I am scared to death."

Dr. Franklin nodded for us to follow him. The three of us sat in a small office behind the nurses' station. I suppose, seeing Melissa shake, he thought we needed coffee. Taking three ceramic cups from a cabinet, he poured the hot soothing liquid. He asked us if we desired cream and sugar to make the coffee more palatable. When he knew we were comfortable, he diverted his eyes to Ralph's chart thumbing through pages of reports.

"Mrs. Garner, the prognosis for Ralph is not good."

"Let me interrupt, Dr. Franklin. Ralph and I are divorced. I am not legally…"

"I know you are divorced. All the information I have is here in his chart but I am allowing you certain privileges. There is a privacy enactment and legally, I can not divulge certain portions of his records. Both of you are aware of his mental conditions as evidenced by his actions on your property but I need to know more in order to help him. Mr. Jenkins, I understand you wish to speak to Mr. Garner."

"Yes, Sir. Melissa asked me if I would. I am not certain how Ralph will react but I am willing."

"Mr. Garner is delusional and appears to be paranoid. Knowing about his continuing outbursts and attempted suicide is paramount to you seeing him. Might the two of you fill me in on his background so I can make a decision for this request?"

"Dr. Franklin," Melissa interjected, "I hope you can help Ralph. Deep inside him is a demon from Vietnam. I don't know if you are aware of the torture Ralph and other soldiers brought back from the war. It doesn't make sense that he and others can't get the help they need. He has lived with continual nightmares from the first day he stepped on Vietnam soil. Coming home, the veteran's should have been given priority in medical assistance."

"You're looking at another war veteran, Mrs. Garner. I know what they went through. I saw the carnage, death, disruption of lives and believe me, I do understand. Look, I may be an ancient old geezer as a doctor, but I still know what it was like and can still be affective with my doctoring. There is no mention, whatsoever, that he was ever in Vietnam. Has he seen other doctors?"

Melissa laughed. "I am sorry to be flippant, but each doctor Ralph went to told him to grow up and put the war behind him, to get on with his life. They put him on medication to calm him down, but never once gave him a medical explanation for his ailment."

"Don't be so judgmental, Mrs. Garner. Ralph never went to the right doctors."

"Excuse me! He did go to the Veteran's Hospital and had numerous exams. He is still waiting on the government to acknowledge his existence. He has mental problems from seeing his friends get blown to hell and having to hold arms and legs ground up like raw meat. You can't tell me there is not a medical need for help."

Dr. Franklin frantically wrote the words Melissa told him. Before Melissa stopped talking, Dr. Franklin had written ten pages of notes. "Mr. Jenkins, it will be alright if you see Ralph. Listening to Melissa blurt out her heart, Ralph needs to talk—talk about what he saw, heard, smelled and felt. There are groups for Veterans but few of them spill the pain or let others know their experiences. It's called the American Vietnam Veteran's Association. If you will come with me, I will take you to his room."

I was uncertain how to talk to Ralph. On a personal level, I didn't know him. I only knew of the destructive behavior he displayed on the front lawn. What would I say to him and how would he react to seeing me with Melissa? Single file, we walked into his room. He was awake.

Dr. Franklin walked to the bedside, taking Ralph's hand in his. "Mr. Garner, I am Dr. Franklin, the attending physician. It seems you have calmed down enough to speak with me and I want you to know, I understand the excruciating pain you are suffering."

Ralph turned to Dr. Franklin, eyes glaring as the words slurred from his mouth. "No you don't. No one understands."

"I do understand. Melissa told me you were a Vietnam Veteran."

"Don't say the word Vietnam. I hate it!"

"I know you do but until you talk about it, you will continue to thrash out at anyone who wants to help you."

"Help me—help me? No one can help me."

"Try to calm down, Mr. Garner. First, I want you to know, your facial trauma is called Bell's palsy. It is a condition making the muscles of the face weak or become paralyzed. The seventh cranial nerve is affected but it is not permanent. You will recover. Did you experience dry eyes or tingling around your mouth several days before your facial droop?"

"Yes. I went to see Melissa to find out why I was so grotesque. She told me the same thing but I didn't believe her."

"She was right, Ralph. It may take several weeks for you to fully recover but gradually you will see improvements. Now we can focus on why you are so belligerent. Your present state of mind needs to be addressed. Do you know Mr. Jenkins?"

"Yes, I do. Why?"

"He would like to talk to you. Are you willing to speak to him?"

"After how I treated him, why should he want to talk to me?"

I walked over to Ralph's bed. "Ralph, I know you don't know me but I am Melissa's friend. She is scared to death—deathly afraid of what you might do. I told her we could get to know one another, if you will agree to it."

Ralph looked at me and then to Melissa. "I am sorry for all the hurt I have caused you. I have a raging devil inside me—one so strong the foothold won't turn loose. I need to talk but I am scared, scared like I was in Vietnam."

"I know nothing about Vietnam, Ralph, but I am willing to listen to anything you want to say. Before we talk about it, tell me about the black wall. Let's go there first. Melissa said you were screaming "black wall" and writing your name. What does it mean?"

"I'm really tired and my stomach hurts. Do you think you could come back tomorrow? Right now, all I want to do is sleep."

"If Dr. Franklin gives permission, I will be back. Will you talk to me?"

Ralph turned his head sideways and whispered, "I'll try."

We left his room, Dr. Franklin wrote a note on Ralph's chart and I knew tomorrow would be a day to remember.

Eight

I was a basket case. In a few short months, my world had been turned upside down. It was hard to believe my happy go lucky personality could be swarmed with death and destruction. My ordinary world was transposed from a tranquil honey comb to a hive of angry bees—bees not of my making. Had I known all this would happen, I might not have been eager for Melissa to enter my solitude. Regardless of what might have been, she was in my life. Ralph was on the verge of self destruction and I was supposed to help him. How could I possible help someone who didn't want to help himself?

Then I thought of my accident; I had the same attitude toward life. Betty helped me when she didn't have to, so now it was my time to return the compassion she showed to me. I might not make Ralph's life perfect but I would try the best I could.

It was 8:00 a.m. and I was procrastinating. To tell the truth, I had no desire to fight parking lot maniacs any more than I wanted to see Ralph. Talking out loud and questioning my ability to get Ralph through another day didn't help, because I came up with the same answer. Just do it.

I arrived at the hospital, armed with questions. The nurse and I went in to Ralph's room. He was sitting upright without restraints. A thought raced around in my head like roller blades. What would I do if he became violent? Would I have the stamina to control the situation or would I belly up? It was too late. I was in his room and watched the nurse shut the door when she left.

Ralph and I stared at one another, not knowing who should make the first move. Blurting out, I began the first commitment. "Good morning, Ralph. How are you today?" He didn't respond. I continued, "Are you sleeping better?" Still no response.

Ralph was moving erratically. His legs shot out from under the sheet and it scared the hell out of me. I didn't know what to expect. To make him feel more comfortable, I moved the courtesy chair closer to the bed. Now, I was at arms length. If he came out of the bed, I was a goner. I didn't care if they labeled me a lily livered yellow crayon, my artificial leg would be moving me right along to the nearest exit. He turned and stared directly into my eyes.

"You're afraid of me, aren't you?"

"To put it bluntly, yes!"

"I can't say I blame you. At least you're honest. I didn't think you would show up here today."

"Do you want to talk?"

"If you think I am going to talk about 'Nam, you're crazier than I am. 'Nam is a subject I can't talk about and I don't want to entertain you with a bunch of chit chat."

"It's the crux of your problems, Ralph."

Ralph hit the mattress with his fist. "Look, you don't know shit about 'Nam. What makes you an authority on the subject?"

"I never said I was enlightened about anything. You're right but until someone tells me what it was like, how do you expect me to converse with you? My dad was in Vietnam and he died over there. At least you're alive."

"I'm not alive. Don't you get it? I am as dead as my friends. Dead! My body is here...I'm not."

"Alright, we don't have to discuss Vietnam. Let's talk about something else."

Ralph snickered. "Something else...let's see. When I get out of here I am looking forward to being locked in a jail. This one room is like a jail without bars. I can't go anywhere, have a smoke or go to the goddamn pot without being escorted to the bathroom. The chair you're sitting in will be removed when you leave. They are trying to protect me from myself. Haven't you seen the guard outside my room? An officer is there 24/7 just waiting to haul me off. As soon as my stomach heals, I'm out of here."

"I've seen him but you need to remember why he was put there."

"I have remembered it for five days. Do I have to show you the holes in my stomach?"

Our conversation or lack of conversation was getting nowhere. Ralph was as hostile as ever and extracting his fears would not happen today. The nurse came in the room with Ralph's meds. She told him to open his mouth while she placed the capsule on his tongue. He took water and she left the room. He put his hand to his mouth and coughed. A few seconds later, he said, "Those damned pills are hard to swallow."

"I know what you mean. When I was in the hospital, pills I had to take were hard to get down. I am surprised you could do it with a little sip of water."

"You get used to it."

"Ralph, I know you have a hard time talking about your problems but will you answer a question? What is the "black wall?"

My question triggered an avalanche. "The black wall is names, names, names and more names. They cover the place as far as the eye can see. Heroes of all sizes and shapes..."

"What does it look like, this black wall?"

"Death! It's a winding path with arms and legs. Its body is hinged inside the earth like a massive giant and it waits patiently for newcomers to come within reach, to lay eyes upon its grandeur. I've seen it one time and I don't want to see it again. I cried till I was exhausted."

"Is it real or something you have manufactured?"

Ralph's demeanor sharpened. "You stupid assed son-of-a-bitch! What's the matter with you? It's real! Have you been sheltered all your life?"

I was becoming defensive. "No," I raised my voice, "I haven't been sheltered all my life and don't call me a son-of-a bitch. My mother was not a bitch. Get it straight, understand? My question to you was valid. You were out of your head when Melissa heard you say it. She doesn't know what you meant any more than I do. Either you want to talk about it or you don't. For once in your life, spit it out. I'm getting tired of pussy footing around with you." I stood up to leave when Ralph motioned for me to sit back down. I continued to stand.

The officer, hearing our raised voices, appeared inside the room. "What's the matter here?"

"Nothing, Sir. It is ok. Ralph and I just had a meeting of the mind. We're fine." The officer shut the door and I sat down.

"Ok, Ralph, I want you to tell me about the black wall. I need to know and so does Melissa. Why were you writing your name?"

For the first time, Ralph's tense body melted into a soft repose. "The wall is real. If I remember correctly, there are 58,245 names on the wall. It includes 1,200 MIA's, POW's and a few others. It's the American Vietnam Veterans Memorial in Washington, D.C. It's the most awesome thing I have ever seen and will reduce you to tears. The first time I saw it, it lunged toward me as if it was alive—alive with the spirits engraved in stone—the spirits from Vietnam. My God, those men and women were heroes—heroes from a forgotten era of hellish war."

Ralph's head drooped, tears pouring from his eyes. I didn't know if I should comment on what he said or wait for him to continue. To break his train of thought would have been disastrous. I waited for him to resume talking. You could have heard a pin drop.

"I've never talked about the monument," Ralph told me. "It's breathtaking to know your friends are etched in stone. Black granite rising up from the ground is more than a tribute. It's their final resting place for the world to see. The names are finite from a distance, like a blur until you approach the wall. All of a sudden, names appear like ghosts reaching out for you to touch, waiting to be embraced by their loved ones. They can't speak except by you putting your hand on a name. Any name you touch…you feel the pain and agony. No one talks when they are there, they only cry. No words can describe how they feel inside. It's a numbing sensation aching to the core of the heart."

"Ralph, I know this is hard for you and if you would like to continue later, I will understand."

"Let me finish. Each of the two black granite walls is two hundred feet long and ten feet below ground at the lowest point. When you approach the park, all you can see is chip marks. When you get close enough, you realize they aren't chip marks but actual names etched with precision. It's serene with shadows dancing on the green grassy park. You might see a 'Nam Veteran there, standing with crutches as he slowly traces names with his fingers. Mothers and fathers weep, knowing it's the only remaining thing they have of their son. You might find a baseball, a worn mitt, a birthday card, flowers or flags placed as a remembrance. It is overwhelming to see families clutching one another, knowing their loved one died in a war. You can't fathom what I feel inside me…what I have dealt with for thirty some odd years. Now Todd, you tell me. Am I crazy?"

I was at a loss for words. All I could say was that I was sorry. Ralph knew I could say nothing because I hadn't experienced what he had. Ralph spoke up. "I think you need to leave now. I can not, nor will not, say any more. Please don't come back, I won't be here."

His statement startled me because I wanted to hear more, to understand what the veteran's went through and how they coped when they came home. I shook his hand and walked out the door. I stopped at the nurses' station to tell them I was leaving.

Waiting for the elevator, I saw the police officer remove the chair from Ralph's room. How sad.

On my ride home I thought about the American Vietnam Veteran's Memorial. Mom and I had planned to see the wall but as usual, it was only a plan—a plan never carried through. I believed Mom really had no desire to see Dad's name etched in the wall.

His name on the cemetery tombstone was all she needed to see and it satisfied her to know she did it for him. There was one more thing I needed to do before I called it a day. I drove home, picked up Patches and we went to the house.

I sat in the car talking to Patches, filling her in on what I wanted to say to Melissa. It was like a practice speech and I didn't want to forget anything Ralph told me. I put the leash on Patches and went inside.

The house looked lonely having been stripped of precious memories but it was necessary. Patches was having a romp on the hard wood floors. I slung her rubber ball across the living room and she slid into the kitchen trying to get a foot hold with her toenails. I laughed out loud and it made matters worse. It gave Patches the impetus to run harder. When she finally got tired, she laid down on a small throw rug near the front door. I went about my search.

Melissa and I had cleaned out the attic, except for the old sewing machine and material. She said she wanted to try her hand at sewing some dresses. I made a key for her to come and go as she pleased. It made her happy to know I trusted her with Dad's faithful sewing machine.

The only thing we didn't clean out was the small crawl space above Mom's closet. Dad had made the secret space to hide his shotgun and pistol. It was out of my reach when I was small. After I was grown, I had no desire to snoop where I had no business. Now, I wanted to snoop— snoop till my heart was satisfied. I wanted to find Dad's letters.

Reaching the crawl space would prove to be a challenge, because it was still out of reach. With all of the furniture in storage, I had to think creatively. I went to the trunk of my car, got my spare crutches and wheeled the old wagon to the bedroom. I would find out what the old crawl space hid

Carefully, standing inside the wagon I raised the crutches and pushed the door open. The makeshift door fell inside the closet and dust flew in all directions. There was at least three feet remaining before I could reach the entrance to the space. I cursed myself for storing all the chairs and decided the only way to get up there would be to go home and fetch a ladder. I spit out a string of expletives, chastising myself for storing all of the stupid-assed chairs. Stupid is as stupid does. I would have to drive home for a ladder. I left Patches asleep on the rug and drove home.

Twenty minutes later, I returned with a ladder. Melissa's car was in the drive. She must be inside. The front door was ajar. Pushing it fully open, I yelled, "Melissa, are you here?" I shut the door and went toward the closet. Something was strange. Patches didn't run to greet me.

"Patches, come here girl. Patches." Patches and Melissa didn't respond. I walked through empty the house with my guts in a knot. Patches' leash was gone. I rushed out the front door screaming for Patches. I heard a faint noise from the side of the house and ran the best I could to find out what was happening.

"Todd, thank God you're here."

"Where's Patches, Melissa?"

"She went under the house."

"What?"

"When I got here to do some sewing, I didn't know she was in the house. I opened the door and she bolted. She saw a cat and the chase was on."

"Are you sure she went under the house?"

"I think so. I'm not sure."

"Mom had lattice work put around the house. I didn't know there was a spot large enough for a critter to craw through. It was erected to keep the skunks from hibernating under there. Melissa, get a flashlight out of my console. Hurry! If Patches and a skunk tangle it's going to take ten gallons of tomato juice to get rid of the odor."

Walking around the side of the house, sure enough, a large gaping hole was visible. I knelt on my knees and peered into the dark underside. "Patches, get out from under there. Here, girl. Patches, come on, Patches."

Melissa handed me the flashlight and I beamed the light. Patches was near the front porch chewing on something. "Patches, come here, girl. Come on, now." Patches wouldn't budge. I stood up and looked at Melissa.

"Now what? This has been a hell of a day and Patches is stuck under the house."

"I'm sorry, Todd. I didn't know she was in the house or I wouldn't have opened the door."

"It's not your fault, Melissa, it's mine. We came here to find the letters. I left her here when I went home to get a ladder."

"Why do you need a ladder?"

"It's a long story and I will tell you after I get Patches out from under the house."

"She didn't kill the cat, did she?"

"I hope not but she's chewing on something. The front lattice will have to come off. I need a hammer. Good grief, all Mom's tools are at my house. Gadzooks, just what I wanted to do, drive back home."

"Would you like for me to go get a hammer? I don't mind doing it."

My voice took on an agitated tone. "You can't. My car is parked behind yours. Stay with Patches. If she pokes her head out of the hole put the leash on her. Sit on her if you have to but don't let her go."

Tears welled up in Melissa's eyes. "Todd, I really am sorry."

She looked like a little child being scolded. I reached over and pulled her close to me. My arms went around her with such a force, that all I could think to do was kiss her. "It's ok, baby. We'll get her out." I went to the car and watched Melissa. She was gently placing her hand to her lips. I felt great.

Another twenty minutes and I was, at long last, removing the lattice work from the front of the house. Patches was watching me closely and made no attempt to I move. It was as though she was enjoying seeing me sweat while I removed rusty nails. Her growl was familiar; a funny little growl she made while chewing on her rubber ball.

"Melissa, did Patches have her rubber ball when she went out the door?"

"I don't think so. She went out so quickly, I didn't realize it was her. She startled me."

"One more nail. I feel like my upper arms have been put through the wringer. When I hit the bed tonight; I may not move for a week. Patches, I guess you know you're in the dog house with me; don't you, girl? You've pulled some stunts but this takes the cake."

Taking the lattice work firmly in my hands, I pulled it free from the ground and base of the porch. Patches was obstinate; unwilling to come from under the house. I looked at Melissa and shrugged. "I can't believe it. She doesn't want to come out."

"Maybe her collar is caught on a nail or something. Don't get impatient with her."

I sat down on the ground and took off my leg. I had to struggle with the strap anchored around my thigh; otherwise I would have been caught with my pants down. "I never thought at my age I would be crawling under this cockeyed house. When I was a kid I used to hide under here and spy on my friends."

Melissa coyly asked, "Did you ever spy on me?"

"You bet I did. You were the cutest girl on the block and I wanted to see what boy you liked best."

"Well? Did you figure it out?"

"No. You were so sassy; I don't think any other boy did either. Melissa, hand me Patches' lease. I think I can reach her neck without falling under here. The hole I dug for my hideout is still here and it's full of water. I don't relish the thought of having to dig my way out of mud."

Inching my way toward Patches, I was able to grab her collar and hook the leash. It did my heart good to see her. She was muddy and hesitant to leave her hiding place. I looked around but didn't see a cat. At least she wasn't devouring some critter. Whatever she was chewing on, didn't chew back. I scolded Patches. "I'll never get you clean." She wasn't interested in listening to me and pulled tightly on the leash. I led her to the back of the house and hosed her down. She would have to shake herself dry.

We went back into the house. I wanted to resume my hunt for the letters. Melissa told me not to come to the attic. She didn't want to feel embarrassed by showing off her newly found hobby…sewing. I promised not to interfere. Patches curled up on the rug and whimpered.

The only thing I found in the small crawl space was Dad's old shotgun and green corroded ammo. His pistol was not there. Mom probably sold the pistol. Just as well, because I had no need for it. My heart sank, realizing the coveted letters were not anywhere to be found. I had nothing. Patch Dimple was gone, the letters and Purple Heart were gone and so were the letters he sent to Mom. My stomach ached with the thought of never reading what he wanted us to know about Vietnam. A sinking feeling put me into a miserable state. I put the ammo into a small paper bag to take to the police station, knowing they could destroy them. The shotgun was put in the trunk of my car. I yelled up the ladder to Melissa and told her Patches and I was going home and to be sure and lock the house when she left.

Her voice echoed down the opening to the attic. "Can't you wait for a few minutes, Todd?"

"I really need to take Patches home. Come on over to my house when you've finished here."

"All right, I won't be too much longer. Have the coffee ready, okay? I have a surprise for you. You won't believe my new dress."

Nine

Patches and I managed to drive home in silence. My mind was on the letters and my heart was consumed with pain. We walked into my kitchen and I filled the coffee pot filter with ground coffee. At least Melissa and I could talk about Ralph while we enjoyed a cup or two. The phone rang.

"Hello, Todd Jenkins speaking."

"Mr. Jenkins, this is Dr. Franklin. I have been trying to reach Melissa Garner."

"What's the problem, Dr. Franklin? Melissa should be here in a few minutes. I can have her phone you when she gets here. Is there something I may do for you?"

"Todd, I know you spoke with Mr. Garner. How was his demeanor when you left his room?"

"He was calm when I left...rather quiet. Why?"

"I'd rather not say right now, Todd, but you and Melissa need to get to the hospital right away."

"Yes, sir, as soon as Melissa gets here, we will be on our way. Should I tell her anything?"

"No. The two of you meet me in the waiting area on the second floor." The phone went dead.

What now? I couldn't go to the hospital with mud caked to my clothing so I went to the bathroom and took a quick shower. Melissa pulled into the drive as I was putting on clean clothes. She was standing in the kitchen, just about

111

to pour a cup a coffee, when I told her about Dr. Franklin's phone call.

"Did Dr. Franklin say anything?"

"Nothing, other than we needed to get to the hospital. He told us to meet him in the second floor waiting room."

"Why second floor? Ralph is on sixth floor."

"I have no idea, Melissa. Maybe Ralph is doing better and they transferred him. I doubt there is anything more to it."

"Did you and Ralph have a good talk?"

"Melissa, he scared me. He was silent for a long time and then began talking about The Wall."

"You mean he told you why he was writing his name on the black wall? What was he talking about?"

"The American Vietnam Veteran's War Memorial Wall. It's in Washington, D.C."

"Oh, I know about the wall but when he was talking, I had no idea he was referring to it. What did he say about it?"

"His description left me wanting to see it. Mom and I had planned to see it but never did go. Do you think we might go…the two of us?"

"It would be my pleasure, Todd Jenkins! What else did Ralph say?"

"I was afraid to interrupt him when he spoke, afraid he wouldn't say anything else."

"Did he…I mean, say anything else?"

"Nothing other than he would be going to jail when he was released. He told me not to come back, he wouldn't be there."

"Oh, I don't think he will be released any way too soon, unless the doctor thinks he is doing well enough to be carted off to jail. His stab wounds were pretty deep. The police would have to administer his meds to keep infection at bay. Do you think Dr. Franklin was able to get him into the Veteran's Hospital? It would be a blessing."

"Melissa, let's change the subject. I am worn out from talking about and with Ralph. How did your dress turn out…is it pretty?"

"I won't get to show you until we go back to your place. It's in the trunk of my car. I think you will be pleasantly surprised. I wouldn't mind sewing with that old machine. It doesn't skip stitches like the new machines do. Would you be willing to sell it to me?"

"Sell it? I'm not sure it's worth selling but I might give it to you."

"Do you mean it?"

"Sure. I can't use the thing. Do you have enough room at your mother's house? It's a big contraption."

"That may be a problem. Mom doesn't have an attic and her small bedrooms won't accommodate it. Maybe it's just wishful thinking to think I could actually have a machine in her house. Oh well, until you sell your mom's house, do you mind me using it?"

"No, not at all. Actually, I have been thinking about moving into her house. Do you think it would be a good idea?"

"I don't see why not. It's larger than yours but you would have to put up a fence for Patches."

"It's settled. I'll do it. When we get things settled with Ralph, I can start moving things over there."

"What will you do with your house? Sell it or keep it?"

I looked at Melissa. "I haven't gotten that far along but when the time comes, I'll make a decision."

We pulled into the parking lot and didn't have a difficult time finding a good place to park. Most of the visitors had gone home for the evening and it was a relief not to battle angry drivers. Melissa put her hand in mine and we went to the second floor. Melissa and I had no commitments to each other but being with her felt right. Her hand in mine seemed perfect.

Dr. Franklin approached us, his face wearied. He thanked us for coming and began explaining the situation. "I know the two of you are wondering why I phoned. It is Ralph and the prognosis does not look good."

Melissa and I stared at each other as we didn't fully understanding the doctor's comment. We knew it would take a while for Ralph's recovery but the doctor's words, "prognosis does not look good" seemed out of place for someone being transferred to another hospital floor.

I piped up. "Ralph seemed stable after our conversation. Perhaps a bit confused but stable. What happened, Dr. Franklin? Ralph appeared better after our talk. He was upset about having to go to jail but was resigned to leaving the hospital. He told me not to come back because he wouldn't be here."

"Ralph was supposed to be discharged tomorrow. The stab wounds he inflicted upon himself were healing nicely, albeit the sutures seemed to pull apart each time his bandage was changed. The nurses were aghast when they went to his room. Ralph had managed to tear the sutures from his stomach and opened the surgical wound. He lost a lot of blood and is in critical condition."

Melissa gasped. "My God, why would he do such a thing?"

"We can only surmise his will to die is greater than his will to live. He was somewhat coherent and told the nurses he picked at the sutures and pounded his stomach with his fist simply because he knew he was going to be transferred to the jail tomorrow. I had a conversation with the officer telling him Ralph's wounds had healed well enough to be released. My hands were tied in regards to his court appearance."

Melissa backed up, pressing her body to the wall to keep from falling. Placing her hands to her mouth, as a small child might do, she lowered her eyes and took a deep breath. "Wasn't there any red flags in his overall mental capacity to justify keeping him a few days longer?"

"No, I am sorry to say. My conversation to him was normal and he was lucid with no radical outbursts or threats. It was a simple doctor to patient talk. He told me he was ready to face the court; take his lumps for what he had done. I told him I was doing what I could do to have the Veteran's Administration review his medical records. He seemed happy to hear the news and told me he was going to change. I have no way of knowing if his "change" was a play on words or he actually meant his lifestyle was in need of repair."

Melissa's voice shook. "When will you know something? How long do you think he will be in intensive care?"

"It's hard to tell. I rushed him into surgery to repair the damage but he lost a lot of blood. He wants to die, Melissa, but I hope it won't be while I am his attending doctor. I refuse to allow him to commit suicide. The only way he will die while I am his doctor is by natural causes, not some idiotic maneuver to stay out of jail. As God is my witness, I will get Ralph the help he needs when he is out of jail."

Melissa's sigh echoed down the narrow hallway. "Finally," Melissa cried. "He'll be able to get some help he needs. Dr. Franklin, there is not much I can do to help. I am not able to access any of his accounts to help with expenditures. How will all of this work?"

"I have set up an appointment with a judge to have you legally declared Power of Attorney."

"You're way out of bounds, Dr. Franklin. I have no desire to be made Power of Attorney and quite frankly, I believe the government should step up to the plate and resume responsibility for Ralph's medical bills. It's their fault he is in the state he is. If he hadn't gone to Vietnam, his emotional state wouldn't be what it is today."

"You can't blame the government for his outbursts."

"The hell I can't! Every doctor he went to told him he didn't experience trauma…to suck it up and be a man."

"He's just one man, Melissa, among thousands of other Vietnam Veterans. Can you explain to me how others have managed to survive?"

"How do you know they are surviving? How do you know what other doctors have told them? If a poll was taken, I would bet all American Vietnam Veterans would say the same thing. No one listens!"

"Are you refusing to be made power of attorney?"

"You bet your sweet life, I am. Ralph went bankrupt after we divorced and I will not incur his debts. While we were married, he spent tons of money on visits to doctors with no help from the government. They told him in order to be qualified for disability, he would have to have proof he was disabled."

"I have some of his medical records on file but they do not indicate he was wounded."

"Heaven help me. Ralph may not have physical scars but his insides are so torn up, nothing can be done to repair them. I can assure you, his Purple Heart is not from playing Tiddlywinks with some two year old whose kick in the shin is the only battle scar you can see."

"Melissa, I was in the war and I know about emotional distress, so don't classify me with unwilling doctors. I am trying to do what is best for Ralph and without your assistance, I may not be successful."

"What you are saying is hogwash. What if Ralph and I were never married? Who would you turn to? Would you manufacture a woman to take on this task?"

"Certainly not but this is a case where you will have beneficial words to say. You saw him when he was at his worst and continue to be a part of his life."

"I'm not a part of his life because I want to be. He won't leave me alone. Ralph has a sister out there somewhere. Why don't you try to find her?"

Dr. Franklin became impatient with Melissa. "You told me you didn't know where she is, so how do you expect me to find her?"

Melissa sat in the chair; head drooped toward the floor. "Dr. Franklin, I am not trying to be difficult. It's just not my desire to become torn apart again. I have been through hell and back with Ralph and it won't stop. When will I be able to live my own life? You have no clue what it was like, living with him."

"Well, you're going to tell me. If you won't do what I have asked of you, at least let me record your experiences. Perhaps with your recount, I can send it with my records when Ralph is transferred."

"I would be willing but how will it help? Will the doctors actually sit down and listen to me rant and rave? I will sound like Ralph. They might consider me a candidate for intuitionalism."

"Believe me, they won't. Wait here until I can find out when my next patient for surgery is scheduled." Dr. Franklin excused himself and returned a few minutes later, "Do you have an hour or so to devote tomorrow morning? Ralph is still in intensive care and I seriously doubt he will be out of the unit any time soon. I want to keep him there to monitor his activity."

"Tomorrow will be fine. Do you think Ralph will try anything?"

"He won't. My mistake the first time was in thinking he was stable. Taking him to the psyche ward was my only option. When he showed no signs of violence, we took off the restraints. It was an error in judgment on my part. I had no other choice because he was well enough to be transported to jail. I believe he planned his second suicide attempt to avoid being released."

"Do you think he will recover from this second round of surgery? Some people have great difficulty with anesthetics and it's rough on the body."

"It's hard to tell. Right now he is sedated and we won't know anything until he is fully conscious. Being a nurse, you know the routine and what it entails. I'm not sure how he will react when he finds out he didn't kill himself. He did a number on his stomach and I can't honestly say he will recover. If the nurses hadn't gone into his room he would have pulled out his intestines and bled to death."

"Don't tell me about it. It's bad enough to know he removed the sutures and gouged open his stomach…it's frightening. Doing what he did…he's begging for help. Don't you see his anguish?"

"I'm not blind, Melissa. He is in a terrible, mind altering condition and this hospital is not outfitted to handle it but we are doing everything possible for him. We have psychotherapists here at the hospital but none, in my opinion, who can reverse Ralph's progression."

"I understand. You've done all you can. It's in Ralph's ballpark now and he will make the ultimate decision of his fate. It's getting late, Dr. Franklin, and there is nothing I can do or change what has been done, but I will be here tomorrow morning to sit and talk with you. Maybe what I have to say will help Ralph or some other desperate Vietnam Veteran. We will just have to wait like we've always done and see if anyone listens."

Melissa and I thanked him for being so frank and left the hospital. The drive back to my place was quiet. Neither one of us knew what to say, nor even if we did, could we change the direction our lives had taken? No! We were thrust head long into a bloody battle between life and death; a grim situation. I wanted to tell Melissa I knew the torture Ralph was experiencing but it would have been a lie. Sure, I had entertained thoughts of suicide when my leg was amputated, but my thoughts didn't contain pictures— pictures Ralph was privy to—pictures of death, destruction and horror his body activated from Nam.

We walked into the house like two zombies drained of emotions—emotions running amok with no viable escape. Melissa collapsed on the sofa, staring into space. I wanted to console her but what would I say? I left her alone to gather her thoughts. Patches curled up beside her as if to say, "I may be a dog but I feel your pain."

As I walked into the kitchen to prepare us something to eat, I glanced back at Melissa and Patches. Melissa had buried her head against Patches and was sobbing. Patches was whining. Patches might have been considered just a dog to some people but she was considerate and compassionate—a quality of grace some people never acquire.

I couldn't figure out anything to fix, so while they napped, I drove to the nearest take out and purchased my favorite food. I hoped it would entice a happier frame of mind. The aroma of nuked, Kentucky Fried Chicken wafting through the doorway roused Melissa from her nap. She and Patches bolted like two little children to the kitchen table. Melissa looked so beautiful; golden hair tossed at random, sleep in her eyes.

I lit candles, not for any sinister plan, but in hopes Melissa would regain a sense of balance to her life. She needed something special to let her know how much she was appreciated. She had given so much, to so many and now it was time to return her generosity.

"Awake, are we? You two were snoring blue streaks."

"I did no such thing, Todd Jenkins! Shame on you for thinking we snore." Melissa patted Patches on the muzzle. "We don't snore, do we, girl? We just breathe deeply."

I laughed. "Sounded like snoring to me but then, maybe it was your stomach growling."

Melissa smiled. "My stomach has been growling for the past several hours. Look at the time! Do you realize we haven't had anything to eat all day?"

"We haven't but Patches devoured the food I put out for her. If she got hungry, I believe she could open the fridge, nuke leftovers and have a seven course meal."

"He's talking about you, Patches. To get even, would you like to crawl back under the house?" Patches barked with vigor. "I think she understood what I said, Todd."

"I have a feeling Patches will resume her vigil under the house. She had something treed and it would be to my advantage to find it before she does. Come on, let's eat before the chicken gets cold. Another round in the microwave and it will be as tough as hardtack."

We began devouring the chicken like condemned prisoners, licking our fingers to get all the morsels. Through bites Melissa asked, "Todd, do you think Ralph will recover?"

"You know what Dr. Franklin told you. He doesn't know anymore than we do and I think it's premature to think of Ralph in the past tense."

"Oh, I'm not thinking past tense."

"Yes, you are Melissa, because I thought the same thing. You need to prepare yourself for the unavoidable future. Ralph could die from what he did to himself."

"I know it. When we're finished eating, will you go with me to my mom's house? I know it's after 10:00 but the papers I saved when Ralph and I were divorced might have his sister's telephone number. I need to find her because deep down, I have this ominous feeling of doom."

"Sure I will. It's unfortunate Ralph and I didn't get to know one another. Our brief talk didn't tell me much about Vietnam but there is so much more I need to know. It has become a passion—a passion to find out what my father experienced. I could kick myself seven ways to sundown for losing Patch Dimple. The letters might have contained something to ease my soul."

Melissa jumped up from the table and ran outside. Her abrupt movement scared me into thinking she had enough of Vietnam, my dribble, Ralph and the world in general. I ran after her. "Melissa, I'm sorry for continuing on a subject you don't want to hear. Melissa..." She didn't respond so I left her alone to reflect on her own inner turmoil. Lord knows we were swarmed in chaos.

Several minutes later, Melissa returned to the kitchen. "Close your eyes, Todd, and don't open them. If you peek, I will get mad."

"I thought you were upset with me. Your dress...you want to show me your new dress. I had forgotten all about it."

"Yes, and don't you laugh, do you hear me? If you laugh, it will make me cry. Are your eyes closed?"

"Closed as closed can get. Are you going to put it on and let me see you in it?"

"I'm only going to hold it up, not put it on. Ready, get set...open your eyes."

My heart fell to my feet and tears leaped from my eyes like a water faucet. All I could say was, "Melissa."

"Well, do you think it is a good replica? Todd, are you okay?"

I wasn't okay; I was astonished from what Melissa had done for me. Taking the beautiful creature from Melissa, I cradled it in my arms like a new born baby. Years of memories swelled inside me with the power of a daffodil heaving a bulb in bloom. "This is the most beautiful sight I have ever seen. How did you ever manage to duplicate my beloved Patch Dimple?

Melissa was grinning from ear to ear. "The picture your mother had in her wallet. You know...the one we found? I took it to a quick processing place and had it blown up. I cut it out and used it for a pattern. This is what I have been making on that old sewing machine."

"Whose teddy bear did you use to attach these gangly feet? Where did you get the material? It is identical to the patches sewn on Patch Dimple."

"Old Teddy Bear was mine when I was a child. Mom kept him all these years and when I pulled him from the cedar chest, I knew what to do with him. Scraps of the leftover material gave me the idea of putting them to good use. I think Patch Dimple II is beautiful."

"I love you, Melissa Garner. I never thought I would say those words to another woman, but I do. I love you more than words can say."

"Are you sure, Todd? Are you sure you aren't saying it just because I made another Patch Dimple?"

"I haven't been surer of anything in my life. You have brought sunshine to my life, not just with Patch Dimple but by your willingness to accept me as I am. How on earth did you manage to find me?"

"Let's call it Devine intervention."

Ten

I finally got to bed around 3:30 a.m. and woke up two hours later. My mind was a myriad of questions. Would Melissa and I marry? Were we premature in declaring our love? How would she and I handle the strain of Ralph's intrusion? Will Melissa prove to have the power in helping Ralph? The foremost question in my mind was would Ralph recover from his second suicide attempt? Question after question engaged me with unanswered resolve.

The previous evening, Melissa and I had sifted through tons of divorce papers in search of the illusive address for Ralph's sister. I was fearful of what her response would be when Melissa made the call. At 2:00 a.m., a curt hello reverberated on the end of the line. As Melissa related the news to her ex-sister-in-law, repose mellowed all the way through her bones. Her posture softened and I waited for her response.

"Oh Todd, she is coming to take care of Ralph's business affairs. It will take her a couple of days to secure someone to cover for her but she will be here. I am so relieved and won't have to continually refuse to be power of attorney."

"You do plan on speaking with Dr. Franklin, don't you? You aren't going to wait until his sister gets here?"

"No, I won't wait but you'd better go home so I can get up in the morning to face my responsibility."

Melissa walked me to my car, gave me a quick peck on the lips and told me to have a good night. She laughed and whispered, "Or should I say, have a good morning, since the evening has disappeared."

~ * ~

While she was with Dr. Franklin, I was going to the bank. Mom's safe deposit key was staring me in the face. Since I had searched the entire house and found nothing, I hoped the safe deposit box would reveal incredible documents connecting me to Dad.

When I entered the bank, Mr. Carrington escorted me to the vault. With pen in hand I scribbled my signature and handed him both keys necessary to open the box. I had been placed on her bank account many years ago, but never intruded on her privacy. My heart raced with eagerness in what the small locked box would contain. Placing both keys into the lock, Mr. Carrington opened the steel door and lifted the box onto a resting table. He told me to be sure to lock the box when I exited.

My heart pounded, knowing I was meddling into her private secrets. I felt like a little kid sneaking a chocolate chip cookie from the cookie jar, rearranging the cookies so the missing one would not leave a void in the container. I thought my feelings could possibly describe a thief as he entered an establishment to burgle. Shaky hands began to unravel a passion she held dear.

I removed the first layer: deeds to the house; payments made to the loan officer. Then I proceeded cautiously to find several love letters from Dad when they were going together. I decided not to read them; putting them aside still bound together with the red ribbon. Beneath those were Valentine cards I had given her and my school report cards. An item leaping out at me was a paper airplane. The paper airplane Dad made for me—the one I thought soared to the moon. Sandwiched inside an envelope was my medical records; mumps, measles and chickenpox vaccination dates. At last, I understood how Mom could rattle off precise moments of my childhood illnesses; she had kept all records of my visits to doctors, as well as those from my hospital stay when my leg was removed. It made me humble and sad to know she spent so much money on me. She was a good mother.

Tears slowly flowed down my face and I thought surely someone would notice because I was not the only person in the bank vault. Thankfully, they were not interested in what my emotions held. I continued with my search.

I lifted an item wrapped inside an old dishtowel. It was Dad's pistol. I held it thinking of the times we went target shooting. I was so small and he was so large and I was sure I would never reach his height. It's frightening to think about, but when you are small and glance upward at a parent, it makes you feel like a small grain of sand, all alone on a vast beach. Glancing at the pistol, I remembered he would never let me hold it without him standing at my side. As I think about it, I probably couldn't have lifted it above my waist. It was heavy.

The next item was bonds. Several of them had matured, so I decided to cash them. I put them inside my shirt pocket and would let my banker handle the transactions. Then I found a marriage license, death certificates of both their parents...and Dad. Once again, I was reduced to tears as I felt a closeness to him, something I hadn't felt for years.

I remembered the gloomy day when the chaplain and military personnel arrived on our doorstep. Years were closing in on me and I could only imagine how life would have been if he had not died in the war. In a way, it was surreal, with thoughts of playing ball, going fishing and doing things only a father and son would do.

The last thing I found was the letters. A flood of emotion captured me like a prisoner of war, peering through barbed wire, waiting for release. I put them inside my pocket, placed all the other items back inside the lock box and closed the chamber. I was eager to go home, read the letters and try to understand the agony he must have felt.

Exiting the bank, Melissa's car was parked next to mine. It implied she had completed her talk with Dr. Franklin. Waltzing proudly from the bank, knowing I had good news for Melissa, my enthusiasm faded. She was wilting over the steering wheel; her body in an uncontrollable sob. I could only imagine Ralph had taken a turn for the worse. My rap on the window startled Melissa and I could tell, from the expression on her face, something was dreadfully wrong. When she saw me, the car door flew open and she collapsed into my arms.

"Melissa, honey, what is the matter? Did it not go well with Dr. Franklin?"

"Take me somewhere, Todd…away from all the hurt and anger."

"Melissa? Talk to me. What's the matter?"

"Ralph died this morning. He went into cardiac arrest while I was speaking with Dr. Franklin. We were sitting in the doctor's lounge discussing Ralph's medical history and how he would make certain Ralph wouldn't be lost in the shuffle. All of a sudden the loud speaker screams *Code Blue, Intensive Care Unit…Dr. Franklin stat*. Over and over the operator announced the Code Blue; an indication of imminent death. He told me to wait in the lounge; he would return depending on the severity of the patient. Thirty minutes later, Dr. Franklin stood in the doorway; his face ashen. His words to me were, "I'm sorry, Melissa. I don't know how to tell you this, but Ralph just passed away."

"Oh, Melissa, I don't know what to say. Did Dr. Franklin say what caused him to go into cardiac arrest?"

"All he told me was the trauma from Ralph's second attempt at suicide probably set it in motion. It's possible a blood clot entered his lungs. He lost a lot of blood when he self inflicted the injury to his previous stomach wounds. The second surgery to repair Ralph's stomach was intensive. I don't know anymore than I did when I left the hospital. I am just so tired—so tired."

"I know you are, Honey. Do you feel like driving to my place? If you don't, I'll tell the bank you are leaving your car in the parking lot so it won't be towed."

"No need to leave it here, I can drive. Yes, I want to go to your house because I don't want to be alone right now. If I go to Mom's house there will be another twenty questions and I am not up to it. My mind is full of unanswered questions and until an autopsy is performed, the questions won't be resolved."

"Did you give Dr. Franklin permission to do the autopsy?"

"Yes. I couldn't wait for Ralph's sister to get here. At this point, I don't think she would harbor any resentments with me saying to go ahead. Please, Todd, no more questions till we get to your house. I can't think straight."

I made Melissa drive ahead of me so I could be assured she didn't veer off into a ditch or wind up wrapped around a telephone pole. I was relieved when she slowly pulled into the driveway. Melissa was spent; her emotions unraveling in countless directions. There was no need to question her or try to make sense of Ralph's death. The only thoughts I had about Ralph was why he was so consumed with death and what could have been so horrid in Vietnam. I knew I might find the answers in those letters; how he felt and what he went through during his tour. I suggested to Melissa, she might feel better and have a better perspective if she took a nap. She didn't hesitate.

While Melissa was napping, the letters burned like wildfire through my mind. Sitting at the kitchen table, I laid the letters in front of me. One by one I picked them up, afraid to peek inside the yellowed envelopes, knowing full well I might crumble with the weight of what he endured. It wasn't cowardice but did I want to read them? Did I really want to reveal a time in his life just to sate my inability to be a soldier? No, it wasn't the reason…I needed closure. Just as the sun comes up in the morning, I was about to get full impact of a blazing fire.

~ * ~

Dear Thelma,

Well, we are in the plane, somewhere over a world of water. It's hard to get my bearings and enjoy the ride. I am afraid to admit it but I am scared to death. This is only my third airplane ride and the ride is not what I thought it would be.

The men and I are huddled together with so many questions about what will happen to us. Some of them are crying. Thelma, they are just little kids—kids pushed into a war they don't understand. I don't understand it either but I won't let them see me cry. In secret, have cried a thousand tears knowing I may never see you and Todd. I am sorry if my letter is so shaky but this plane is bumpy with all the turbulence.

Before we left the States, our Sergeant told us some of us would not be coming home and I know he's telling the truth. I have heard bad stories about Vietnam and I don't know what to expect. I don't want to scare you but you need to be prepared for the worst. I have set up my allotment to come straight to you, except for a few dollars. I don't know if I will need money or not. They didn't tell us but a few dollars is all I need. Go to the bank and see if you can have someone go over our account. I know we don't have a lot of money but maybe they will work with you knowing I have gone to war. Don't let them run over you. Hold your ground like you do with me.

Sweetheart, it's getting dark and I need to get some shut eye. It won't be long before we touch ground. I love you, Thelma, and miss you. Tell Todd Jr. how much I love and miss him...he's our anchor, Thelma. God, I miss you so. Say prayers for me and all the rest.

My love...

My hands shook while the tension in my neck felt like a vise ready to implode. Thoughts of my father, realizing he might die were more than I could bear. He must have been terribly frightened hearing that some of them would not come home. Dying a natural death, among those you love in familiar territory, is hard enough to grasp but to have it drilled into your head that none of your family members will be with you, is gut wrenching. I could only imagine how the rest of the troops felt. Laying the letter aside, I picked up the next one, unaware of the harrowing content.

~ * ~

My loving, Thelma,

We are in a little town north of Saigon. I have been here for a couple of days getting oriented to the surroundings. We have had many things to do. Our Sergeant is a massive man, not one to put up with slacking. The first day we were here, we were put through the most horrid but effective drills. The live ammo whizzing above our heads made us realize our immortality. This is real, Thelma, they're shooting real bullets. Crawling through the barbed wire, afraid to look up, scared me bad...really bad. I know it was for my own good and it was an exercise to show us what will be next but God, I can't believe what might happen.

Saigon could be a beautiful place but right now, nothing is beautiful. The dirt and grime is appalling and the noise is ghastly. The odor is dreadful and seeing little kids run around without clothes makes me sick to my stomach. Street corners harbor women whose desire is to trap a soldier. I am sure some of them are desperate for survival. It doesn't get any better with time. I am afraid to tell you but some of the women are enemies. Don't worry, Honey, I won't be lured into their trap. I am doing a job for my country and it doesn't include what the women want. You are my life, Thelma, my breath...my reason for living. I've got to go, Thelma. The Sergeant is screaming orders. I love you, Baby. Kiss Todd Jr. for me. The letters may be far and few between as I leave tomorrow on a mission. I miss you so much. Please say prayers for us.

Your loving husband

~ * ~

The intensity of the second letter, with him knowing he would be in close proximity to the enemy must have cut to the bone. Fear must have gripped at his throat.

I was having breathing spasms and my mouth felt like a wad of cotton-balls. My heart was trying to race from my body. Cautiously moving my chair, I rose to get a cup of coffee. Not wanting to wake Melissa, but needing to share with her my new found bounty, I ventured a stare toward the living room couch. She was sleeping peacefully. Somehow these letters might shed light on Ralph's desire to die, but now was not the time to infringe upon her space. Sharing would have to wait. Several hours passed while perusing the letters. Most of them were the same, sans one. It was as gruesome as death itself.

~ * ~

My darling, Thelma,

It is now sunrise and I have been awake for the better part of the night. Catnaps here and there are all we can manage. Charlie is always there and we don't dare sleep for fear of dying. Destruction is at an all time high. Holes from bombs ravage the entire area, concertina wire and bodies lay everywhere. It is the most awful sight I have ever seen. Perhaps I should not be telling you the terrible truth but you need to know. My heart is heavy with grief as I held a dying friend in my arms. It is so chaotic here with napalm searing the flesh with third degree burns and sometimes leaving a body unrecognizable. So many bombs have exploded shattering legs and arms or decapitating those in its wake that I can't bear to see another human go through such torture. Terror is at an all time high because of the ruthless acts of murder. It is murder, Thelma, murder to see a friend be ripped apart for a senseless war...a war never having been declared by our country. It is a shame our young men have been sent to this country to fight a non ending war. Many people will die today, some of them my close personal friends. Goddamn it, Thelma, this fuckin' war is sheer hell. I don't want to die in this God forsaken hellhole for the piss assed government who thinks they know what they are doing. I'd like to ram my fist down all the idiot's throats and jerk out their guts. Maybe the motherfuckers would get a taste of what we are going through.

This filthy place is a bitch! It's Goddamn impossible to sleep in this rat infested hole and when I am able to get some Z's, it's nothing but maggoty nightmares. Hell, I don't even know what I am saying...my mind is all fucked up. I saw a person die...and it was me. It was my death, Thelma, my own Goddamn death, smeared with blood and guts. I was trying to put myself back together but nothing I did seemed to help. My body lay there in a heap of burned flesh and my intestines were rotting right before my eyes. My fingers were long and boney. No skin was attached and each time I tried to pick something up, the bones would fall in a heap. God, Thelma, I think I am losing my mind! Maybe it was an omen for things to come because God is my witness, this dream was real. I don't know if it was from seeing everything, day in and day out from this awful ritual of death and destruction but whatever it was, I can't take much more. Baby, you may not get this letter but it sure felt good to write it. If I see it on paper, maybe it will get out of my mind.

Some of my friends have gone off the deep end. They talk of being in a zombie like state, pulling the veins of dead men from their bodies and tying up the enemy. Thoughts of suicide creep into their minds. Death runs deep as an ocean and the smell of stiff, decapitated rotting corpses linger on our clothes. You can't wash it off, no matter how hard you try. We don't have a bath too often and having the guts of men stuck inside and out of our combat gear, inside our helmets and boots is more than we can bear. The stench is overwhelming and is enough to put you over the edge. I puke all the time and it feels like bugs are crawling all over me, eating away at my flesh. My mind is playing tricks and I can't seem to stop it. I am hounded with living nightmares while I am awake and vivid ghoulish nightmares when I am finally able to fall sleep.

Being in the trenches for two weeks at a time is God-awful. Terrible booby traps are hidden in the trees, waiting...waiting to snatch the life from us. I saw one man hit in the chest, his intestines splattered from the bottom of the tree to the limbs hanging above our heads. Part of him was dangling in mid air. We couldn't get what was left of him down. Charlie wouldn't let us. By the time Charlie was finished with him...nothing and I do mean nothing was left of his body. We couldn't even get close to his dog tags without ammo killing one of us. By the time we were able to retrieve the dog tags, it was nothing more than a piece of tangled metal. You couldn't even read the name of the dead soldier. I can still see it in my mind and it is slowly killing me. I wish I could have helped him, but God help me I couldn't. No one could, Thelma, no one could. I think about his family and other families' torn apart by this tragedy. They are sons, husbands, fathers or relatives dying—dying—for what?

I think I am becoming paranoid, Thelma. When we are back at base, I see things—things coming at me in all directions. The top of the tents crawl with black dots—dots with gnarly fingers wrapped in bandages and blood. Eyes are vicious with fire dancing in the background. It's like millions of fireflies doused with gasoline going up in a ball of fire, chasing, chasing, chasing me to get a death grip. Sometimes I wake up in a cold sweat, screaming out for help. Then I realize I am not in a trench or in the bush but on a cot.

Pulling the army blanket above my head to stop the screams suffocates me in a way no one understands except for those going through the same agony. I sometimes think death would be a pleasure, to erase the memory of seeing all the tragic events. I hate this place, Thelma, I hate this place. I hate what it has done to me, what it has done to you and Todd and what it has done to all my comrades and their families. I want to come home to you. I want to hold you in my arms. I want to play with Todd, eat a good meal and sleep. Actually sleep in a bed without wondering if the world will come to an end.

I am sorry to burden you with so many complaints, and dreadfully sorry to blurt out what is inside me. You and Todd are my only source of sanity and I can't wait until I get home. Only two more months of this hell hole and I will be home. This is the longest letter I have written but it is the most important. I want you to know, if I don't make it home...forgive me. Things are beginning to heat up around here so I'd better close for now. I love you and Todd Jr. so much. Maybe soon, I will see you. Until then, keep praying for me. Hugs and kisses xoxoxo

~ * ~

I couldn't believe what I had just read. It's no wonder men of the Vietnam War have suffered tremendous illnesses. Their peace of mind was snuffed like a child with a head cold. Mother was right about the insanity returning Veteran's had to encounter. It wasn't so much from listening to men talk but from reading all these letters. She knew he would not be the same, no matter what she tried to do. Even if he came home from the war, his mental outlook and nightmares would have created a chasm of pain and possibly paranoia...and suicide. Bundling the letters into a pile, I knew what I had to do. My next step was to verify what I had read...somehow find a living American Vietnam Veteran who might shed more light on the atrocity of Vietnam. Until Ralph's funeral, plus all the other things taking precedence within our lives was finalized and put to rest, only then our lives would find a more meaningful existence. The American Vietnam Veteran's Association would be my next line of communication.

Eleven

Two weeks later after Ralph's funeral, things started to calm down. Our emotions were topsy-turvy getting things in order. Death certificates, faxing documents to state agencies and duplicate copies piled as high as our ankles. Dying left a bitter taste in my mouth, not because of succumbing to a natural step in life but for the magnitude of what it entailed.

The autopsy report, mandatory in most states, brought to light what we thought to be true. Ralph's death was in fact from a heart attack but it also found pieces of shrapnel inside his body. He was a virtual piece of metal; trapped like a time bomb ready to explode. Tiny flecks dotted his brain cells with ballooning veins ready to erupt. Had the heart attack not killed him, his head would have evaporated into a wave of blood.

We had no way of knowing how long he would have lived, or if his paranoid actions, far exceeding the outbursts we were subject to seeing, would continue. He also was a diabetic prone to blood sugars whose values exceeded the mark at two hundred. At any moment he could have gone into a diabetic coma. Why he was never diagnosed was a question none of us could fathom. Perhaps if he had gotten the proper medical attention, Ralph would still be living.

Like everything else Ralph had done, we could only surmise the outcome. We would never know.

My loss with the death of Ralph was devastating. My hopes were to reach inside him and extract visions he encountered. I wanted to tell him about my wish to die when my leg was amputated...to make him understand he wasn't the only person in the world whose life had been shattered.

Circumstances surround people in everyday occurrences, some horrendous, but we learn to live with them. My chance to reach him stopped too abruptly. The letters I had read would not reach him nor would they let him know how valued a person he was in his attempt to keep Americans safe from harm. Ralph's death, like all the other American Vietnam Veteran deaths were not in vain. They were to be honored and held in high regard for service above and beyond the call of duty.

I guess the thing upsetting me most is Ralph would not meet Tommy J. Moon, a survivor of the Vietnam War, a real honest to God fighter whose penchant for living demanded his full attention. My phone call to the American Vietnam Veterans Association put me in touch with Tommy and I set up a time to meet with him; to learn about his personal battle and the battle he fought.

~ * ~

CPL Moon, Tommy J., 13B40, Battery B, 20 Battalion 11th Artillery, 101st Airborne Division. (Airmobile.).

It was easy to recognize Tommy J. Moon as I walked into Denny's Restaurant in Fort Smith, Arkansas on January 4, 2005. A proud man, he wore a ball cap decorated with Veteran memorabilia and sat alone in a booth. When I approached him, he stood as any gentleman would; extending his hand as a welcoming gesture. His firm grip let me know immediately he was taught good manners.

I introduced myself and explained why I wanted to

speak with him. "I need to know what my father experienced in Vietnam. I hope you do not mind telling me your story."

We ordered coffee and then began our conversation. As I found out, he would have no trouble spilling his thoughts into a tape recorder, although his first glance at the recorder was less than enthusiastic. I knew he was eager to tell his story—a story put on the back burner, but scared to spill his guts. I could tell it would be a difficult for him to open up, but he cleared his throat several times, looked at me through misty eyes, and revealed his tormented soul.

I listened intently to Tommy J. Moon as he recalled torturous details of his stint in the Vietnam War. His face, sometimes drawn while reflecting, revealed saddened eyes and a nervous twitch. His experience as an American soldier fighting the war in Vietnam was not a story many Americans wanted to hear, especially a war they never embraced.

When the interview concluded, I raced back home. My stomach was in knots and my body shook uncontrollably. It was the first time in my life to listen to a story so gruesome, it left me in turmoil. I was eager to re-play and listen to the taped account of Tommy's story. Sad to say, I was dismayed at the quality of the interview. Coffee cups and dishes clanking in the background, people conversing in other booths, and shuffling of feet overpowered this marvelous man's recollection. Putting my memory to the test, I began the task of writing what he said. I had to put in on paper so I wouldn't forget a word. It was a burning urgency. As I relate Tommy's story to you, I hope his story and other American Vietnam Veteran stories will let you understand the continuing war within their heart, souls, and mind. Tommy began.

~ * ~

"I was young, twenty two to be exact," Tommy said with a powerful determination etched across his face. "It was 1968. In Hooks, Texas, I worked six months for Lone Star, an ammo plant, thinking I would be there forever. It was a good job and I hoped it would be my life's career. It was a normal day, just like always; until I saw my father approach me. I had no idea why he was there but soon found out. "Tommy, this letter came today. It's for you and is important. You'd better read it. It's a draft notice from the United States Government." I didn't know what to think but I took the letter from him and stared at it.

I knew what I had to do. Back then, if you loved this great country—my country, the United States of America—you served the Armed Forces with pride. The letter was from Uncle Sam, drafting me into the military. No, sir! No draft letter for me. I marched myself into the local recruiter's office, handed him my letter of draft and told him I was enlisting…volunteering before my draft date.

No Moon family member ever had to be told to do something, we just did it. It's the kind of stock inside my veins—proud stock. Of course, at age twenty two, what man thinks they aren't invincible? None of us knew what lay before us; where Vietnam was. All of us draftees or volunteers knew was that Uncle Sam needed us. We were proud to be Americans and proud to serve our country."

Taking a sip of coffee, he continued. "The following Monday after receiving my draft notice, I packed my bags, told my parents goodbye and left my home town of Pasadena, Texas to attend basic training in Ft Bliss, Texas. I was now the property of the United States Government. I would learn hand to hand combat, run obstacle courses and learn how to put together an M16 rifle blindfolded. I had to learn many things and learn well. If the Army told you to do something, you did it. No questions asked. Infantry training was grueling but necessary to survive the enemy forces I would encounter.

From there, I was in Redeye Gunnery training at Fort Riley, Kansas. A redeye anti-aircraft missile is a short range shoulder fired missile launcher. In fact, I knew all the military equipment—front and back and everything in the middle: M-14 rifles, M-203 Grenade Launchers, Thompson Sub Machine Guns, M-1/M-2 Carbine Rifles…you name it, I knew how to do it. The list goes on and on. I got this training at AIT at Fort Hood, Texas. It was Advanced Training in artillery dismantlement and other military machinery and from there I went to Fort Sill, Oklahoma.

Exactly one year later, from the day I received the draft letter, I had managed to learn many things for survival—or so I hoped. Although I was old enough to vote and buy liquor, some of us were still considered kids. The average age of the American Vietnam War soldier was nineteen years, five months and eighteen days. Even at nineteen, most of us were still green behind the ears and didn't have a care in the world. We woke up in a hurry.

Yeah, we weren't old enough to legally vote or buy liquor; but God help us; we were old enough to die for our country. Times haven't changed much. Training is the basically the same, only they have more advanced weaponry—computer warfare. All the computers in the world won't stop the hand to hand combat. It only allows the ground forces to know exact perimeters. It's a given. It's a fact. In war we die for our country.

After orientation, we left San Francisco, California on the long trip to a land I couldn't even spell, Vietnam. It was a cold January morning when we boarded a Tiger Jet, a smaller version of the Boeing 747. The plane carried only passengers—soldiers heading for Vietnam. We were dressed in our khaki uniforms and field jackets. We did not know one another personally but knew, from our military dress, each of us was headed in the same direction. It seemed as though we were in the air for days, especially for me, since I had never been away from my home or parents. I have to admit, all of us were scared.

Our Tiger jet landed in Da Nang, Vietnam. One by one we disembarked the jet. The moment our feet hit the ground, the heat was so intense sweat poured from our brows. It was like stepping into a sauna. We went from California cold to Vietnam hot. In a matter of minutes, our clothes dripped with perspiration.

The entire area was revolting and I will never forget the stench. It smelled like thousands of outdoor toilets and made me sick to my stomach. The noise and dust from all the heavy military equipment was unbearable. You couldn't take a deep breath of fresh air because the atmosphere was covered with sickening odors. This was just the beginning and we were in for more rude awakenings.

Another barrier was the language. We couldn't understand them and the majority of them couldn't understand us. Regardless of our different nationalities, we managed to convey what we were saying. Sure, we picked up words and understood enough basics to get our meanings across to each other, but still had no idea who was friend or foe. The only true thing we had in common was death. We all knew death.

After the initial shock of realizing we were in a war filled nation, we were shuffled to a large tent. It was an Army compound covering an area of roughly five hundred yards. Sergeants, corporals, captains and E6's were there to greet us. The Army personnel and surroundings were intimidating. We were scared to death, homesick and wanted to cry but we sucked up our tears, gritted our teeth, and listened to every word coming from their mouths. Listen to them or die. One profound statement we all heard was; *most of us would not be going home to our loved ones.* Reality kicked in. Some of us would die a horrible death.

Next on our agenda was an obstacle course. It was not an ordinary obstacle course; one you might drive a go cart through. This was made of concertina wire (barbed wire) and the razor sharp barbs could be deadly if you got caught inside it. We lay on our stomachs, doing a low crawl through trenches made of concertina. It was three inches deep, one hundred fifty feet long and wide enough for one person at a time to crawl through. Above our heads whizzed live M60 shells.

The M60 was considered a general machine gun but proved itself in combat zones. It could fire up to five hundred fifty high-velocity bullets from a gas-powered belt at a time. Its range of fire was over nineteen hundred yards. Sixty rounds of machinegun fire dared us to lift our heads as we made our way along the three inch trench. It was terrifying to know our own government was using live ammo; not wanting to kill us but to show us what to be prepared for in jungle warfare. Nothing on God's green earth could prepare us for what lay ahead.

When I say jungle—I mean jungle. Where we would be fighting, each square inch of it was jungle. Briars entangled with trees, scrub brush so thick you couldn't see through it and mine fields—tons of mine fields dotted the landscape.

The standard mines used by the Viet Cong, was provided by China and the Soviet Union. If they needed more, they would dig up and reuse American land mines, steal Claymore mines from tripods or cut open unexploded bombs. A lot of enemy soldiers were killed by doing this procedure. Their objective was the components inside the mines. They wanted them for their handmade weapons. Traps of various degrees were set to pummel a body with spikes, decapitate or blow skin from body. The horror of it all was seeing someone hacked to death with wooden spikes, permeating the heart with such a thrust it exploded on impact.

North Vietnam forces used deadly homemade booby traps. Sharpened bamboo sticks, called "punji sticks" were secreted in earth pits. They were designed to maim the feet of American soldiers, rendering them helpless. Unsuspecting American soldiers, triggering tripwires, were subject to "bamboo maces," a device the North Vietnamese hung in trees to swing down and pierce bodies. Tripwire crossbows and studded nail boards were other devices used by the enemy. It was a massive killing field without the clearing.

My first experience in combat came when we were leaving Bastogne, North of Saigon but below the DMZ (Demilitarized Zone.) We were on board a CH50 Helicopter, a 101st Air Mobile. Fifteen to twenty men hovered inside the helicopter like sardines in a can, wondering what would happen next. All of us were attached to different units but united with a cause; we were one in spirit.

Incoming VC (Charlie or Viet Cong Soldiers) tried to hit everything and zero in on all firing points. The only way to secure a landing pad was to make the LZ (landing zone) cold. By cold, I mean a prepped area safe for landing. Before a helicopter could land or hover, CB's (Bulldozers) would plow under a killing zone (clearing or open area) of thirty feet. The helicopter would hover and the men would jump out.

Deploying the helicopter, we had to jump three to five feet with our equipment and M16 while wearing our flight jacket and steel helmet. An AK47 would fire around us, allowing us to run three hundred yards. As fast as we could, we would dig a foxhole three feet deep while, at the same time, filling empty sandbags with the dirt and rocks from our beloved sanctuary—the foxhole. We didn't mess around with our incentive, as it only took Charlie three seconds to kill any one of us. Ninety percent of the time the cold areas would be hot as Charlie was all over, waiting to pluck us with bullets.

Two weeks out and two weeks in made us a nervous wreck. It was continuous—night or day. We had no idea when someone would yell, "Let's roll!" We would fly from Bastogne to different areas. It didn't matter which direction we took—it still consisted of two weeks of fighting hell.

I wound up on the Ho Chi Minh Trail close to the Mekong Delta. My God, it was nothing more than a maze of jungle paths being used by the communists to get food and supplies to the VC. One trail would be shut down and another would open. It was like fingers on your hand—get one blown off and four more took its place. Gun fire was at an all time high, blazing with M16's, Howitzers and other high powered machinery to disconnect the supply line. VC swarmed the area like flies.

It was May 6, 1970. We were in the province of Quang Tri. My friend and I were scanning the perimeter for enemies. We were looking through starlight scopes capable of detecting movement at night. Trip wires on the concertina activated and I saw members of the North Vietnamese army approach. We waited until they were across the wire. I hit the clacker on the Claymore mines and the plunger to detonate the gas drum. I saw the VC/NVA being burned alive as they rushed through our perimeter. Dead bodies lined the concertina wire, making it easy for the Viet Cong and North Vietnamese Army to advance forward. One by one, as the enemy fell, their bodies were tossed in random; used as a bridge of death to advance toward American soldiers.

The flesh—God awful burning flesh drifted in all directions. The smells were nauseating—gut wrenching nauseating. "We can't hold them any longer; fall back, fall back," echoed his words through the midst hell blazing gunfire. No one knew whose voice screamed the directive. We felt the ammo from AK-47's rip through sandbags, sending powdery dirt and rocks through the air.

The sandbags, sometimes three and four feet high, were filled with the dirt we shoveled from our fox holes, and without them we were like sitting ducks, waiting to be killed. The hot ammo ground like a meat grinder. It devoured and pierced, churning like a massive giant tidal wave in its wake. Rounds of ammo penetrated the area and you could feel the air burn in and around us. At that point, our mission was to get out of the foxhole before we were killed. We were being overrun by the enemy.

Retreating at least one hundred feet from our foxhole, my buddy was hit by shrapnel from a mortar round. As I turned around to grab him, blood was gushing from his mouth; his eyes wide open. I knew he was dead. My friend, my companion was dead.

We were in panic. Pandemonium raged upon us as we waged combat—fierce combat—soldier against soldier. I ran back to my unit to help the crew of men manning the enormous 155mm Howitzer. A Viet Cong Soldier came running toward the Howitzer with a satchel charge. Realizing what he had in his hand, I was thrown into the air by the force of the exploding satchel bomb. I knew what was happening but it was in slow motion, as if tons of water was rushing above your head—drop by drop—drowning you as a trickle. It was there but you couldn't stop or control it. The concussion of the exploding satchel charge was like being hit in the head over and over with a two-by four. The percussion deafened me.

Dazed, I tried to anchor my body on my knees. As I looked around through blurred eyes, the gun unit was gone. It was as though I was in a cemetery of dead bodies—dead bodies one on one. Fear clutched my throat as a Viet Cong soldier stood above me, glaring down with hatred. I could feel his searing breath but couldn't hear the words he was screaming. Deafness, I thought, wouldn't allow me to hear the bullet taking my life. His AK-47 rifle aimed at my head. Even through blurred eyes, my mind had no trouble looking down the rifle barrel. I knew death was imminent and prayed to God, it would be swift. He pulled the trigger. Nothing! A miss-fire from his gun, a jam or empty cylinder was the only thing between me and death. Out of the blue, he back handed the rifle butt in my left jaw, shattering teeth and bone.

When I awoke from this reign of terror, blood from my body was splattered like raindrops; the pain was excruciating. I was deaf and part of my face had been shattered. I don't know when I passed out or how long I laid there.

I thought I was being dragged but by whom? Was I dead? I didn't know, but I felt as though I was floating to heaven. Clouds were above me, zipping past; taunting me. I felt my feet dangling in mid air and I could smell fresh baking bread and wood smoke from a fireplace. My mind floated with the face of my mother—my wonderful mother so far away and safe from harm. To see all of these blessed things, I surely must be dead. Later, I was told medics dragged me to a waiting CH-50 helicopter, transporting me to triage (mash unit.) I don't remember how long I was out, but the good doctors patched me up.

One day while I was waiting for a doctor to check out my injuries, I saw many mangled bodies. Blood poured from gaping wounds; arms and legs pulverized like ground beef with bone and sinew hanging by a piece of skin, faces obliterated, stomachs ripped apart and the silent screams were overwhelming. My hearing hadn't completely returned but I knew. I knew expressions on their faces were screams. I could barely move my neck but I told the doctor to tend to those persons; they needed care more than I did.

After I was well enough, I returned to my unit. I learned at a later date, through chain of command, thirty-five hundred VC/NVA were killed on that day. I don't know how they arrived at the number. It was probably just an estimate. A friend told me we suffered thirty percent casualties on that God awful day.

Another incident was on 27, May, 1970 in Thua Thien. The ammo dump consisted of every kind of artillery shells. Tons of it sat on wooden supports surrounded and covered by sand bags. The color of the sand bags gave the image of an ordinary landscape. It was our home away from home and if we were lucky, we could grab a few needed winks.

On this particular day, enemy fire was targeting dangerously close to our ammo dump. Dangerous became deadly serious when one round slammed into the ground just inches away from the ammo. The impact sent sparks into the camouflaged compound. All of a sudden, fire raged all around us. Some of the men and I ran to put out the fire before it reached the ammo. It was futile. A guy from engineering drove a bull dozer near the ammo, trying in vain to extinguish the blazes.

Our LT screamed, "Get away, it's going to blow." We ran as fast as we could to take cover. Our LT friend and comrade didn't have a chance. The ammo exploded in all directions, killing him instantly. He didn't know what hit him."

Tommy shuffled his feet under the booth, took a drag off his cigarette blowing smoke rings into the air, and sighed. "No one felt at ease. Thirty hours of no sleep or rest took its toll on many of us. We were exhausted, hungry, angry and anxious. Tempers flared but it was to be expected as we were subject to horrendous situations. The enemy was all around us, hovering like mosquitoes. They were adept in hiding in unsuspecting places.

One thing after the other bombarded us making us dodge all kinds of treacherous elements. If it wasn't bombs or the heat, it was rain. The monsoon season lasted six damned months creating a steam bath all around us. Massive amounts of rain made mud so thick, you couldn't you couldn't scrape it from the soles of your boots. Mosquitoes fed from our perspiration and they were impossible to thwart.

Something else was just as dangerous. There were snakes but I left them alone! Yeah, there were poisonous snakes but not any different from the American Diamondback Rattle Snake. I heard there was a Two-step snake (take one step, get struck and the other step you were dead) but I never knew of one soldier dying from a snake bite. Hell, it wasn't the damned snakes we were worried about, it was the deadly VC. We didn't have time to worry about snakes, we worried about staying alive. Needless to say, somewhere in the backs of our minds the fear was there. On top of knowing about snakes, we were anxious and hot as hell. Even though it was raining, the humidity was so bad; water poured from our faces. It was as though someone turned on a water faucet. The temperature, rain and humidity were scorching.

Fungus on our bodies erupted like sores on a leper. We were told to keep a clean pair of socks to alleviate fungus rot on our feet, but it was impossible. Once a fungus managed to invade your skin, it was like millions of blisters popping at one time. It itched and burned like fire from a raging inferno, all at the same time. Nothing was immune to the humidity. You could literally wring water from our supposedly dry socks.

A bath, if we had one, was maybe once a week if we were lucky. An Australian Bag, with holes in the bottom, held five gallons of water. It had a long tube at the top to pour in the water. Five minutes is all the time we had to step under the cold water, lather our bodies, rinse and get clothed. Sometimes if we were desperate for a bath, a hand grenade would be tossed into a rice patty to expose the water and blow up any mines carefully placed by the VC. Knowing or hoping and praying to God it was secure, several of us would jump in while guards with M-16's took watch. Then we would exchange places. AT least we were able to eradicate some of the filth adhering to our skin and clothing. But, we were always on alert because we had no idea who was lurking in the shadows.

Before we knew it, our two weeks out was up, and another unit would take our place on the firing line. Then we would fly back to Bastogne for our two weeks in. It felt like heaven to be away from death.

There was never a minute we didn't need to be on guard, even at base. Safety was always an issue. VC would infiltrate, pretending to be one of us. I remember one of the Vietnamese cutting my hair. He had been around for awhile doing odd jobs and managed to convince us not to worry. We thought he was one of the good guys. Not so. He was seen around the mess hall, eyeing the perimeter. He would step off and count, getting exact locations for the VC. We caught him in black pajama's hiding in the concertina next to the routine mess hall (a field truck) but we were ordered not to shoot him.

Army soldiers were told never to fire upon anyone without provocation. We were provoked but he was unarmed. We had a choice—kill him and be subject to a court-martial, stripped of rank and jailed or obey orders. Either way, our choice was doomed. On one hand, we fought enemies in our everyday existence; some with weapons, the others with sheer willpower to survive a hell hole of death. We found out the so called good guy had been giving the VC ordinances, C-rations and other items to be used by us— American Soldiers. If it wasn't one damned thing to fight, it was another.

Agent Orange was another hazard. Approximately twenty million gallons of Agent Orange (herbicide) was used to defoliate the jungle mass. It literally burned leaves from trees. Although it killed all plant life to leave Charlie without cover, it also played a major roll in various diseases

American Soldiers would have to contend with when they returned to America.

At present time, according to the Department of Veteran Affairs, there is considerable research being done to learn about the long-term effects of Agent Orange exposure. There are eleven conditions linked to Agent Orange. The conditions, I am told, are: Type 2 Diabetes, Chronic Lymphocytic Leukemia, Multiple Myeloma, Prostrate Cancer, Respiratory Cancers and Soft-Tissue Sarcoma, Non-Hodgkin's Lymphoma, Hodgkin's disease, Porphyria Cutanea Tarda, Chloracne, and Acute and Sub acute Peripheral Neuropathy. None of us were alert to the dangers of Agent Orange. We knew what it could do to plant life but not to us. We didn't have time to worry about walking through the residue or breathing in its poison. We were too worried about getting killed. All we wanted to do was stay alive, do the job we were told to do and return home in one piece.

For some, one piece wasn't possible. Many of the soldiers came home as paraplegics. God, it was an awful sight to see. Arms and legs ripped from the body; men on crutches patched up the best way possible. Heads bandaged to prevent jaws from gaping open and blinded men wondering how in hell they would survive when they got home. All of them worried about supporting their families. They had no viable body parts to maintain a job. We were all caught up in a nightmare with no escape.

The nightmare continued day and night. When we were asleep, memories would crash down upon us like a ravaging mountain of fear—an avalanche of gruesome fear. I remember screaming out, telling men to get to safety. Men with no faces would scream at me in agony. When I reached out for them in my sleep, I would be holding guts in my hands. I thought I was losing my mind. I couldn't get rid of them by day and at night they returned to continue their vigil of haunting.

When my duty was up in Vietnam, I shouted to the high Heavens—I was going home. I couldn't wait to get to America—my wonderful country. It would be wonderful to step upon the land of my ancestry, to see my parents and pick up where I left off. I was anxious for some good home cooked meals. When we landed in Hawaii, we were not allowed to go to the airport lobby. We were ushered straight to debriefing. We were warned to put the Vietnam War behind us. Forget it. How the hell were we to forget the hell we just went through? They told us the war in Vietnam wasn't too popular in the States. That was an understatement.

All the time we were fighting and being killed, protestors were having a flag burning frenzy. We didn't have a clue. We knew nothing about the protest. We were never told. Flag burning by protestors sickened my stomach. Sure there were those people who thought we had no business in Vietnam and I often wondered the same thing but I would never have burned our flag. They were burning the same stars and stripes flag, hailed as our Flag of Freedom, watching and booing as they lay draped across our dead soldiers caskets. It was a travesty.

When I reached San Francisco, I was on my way to the ticket counter to purchase an airplane ticket to Houston. I was wearing my fatigues and my duffel bag slung over my shoulder. Out of the blue, a wild, long haired hippy began yelling at the top of his lungs, "Baby Killer!" The full brunt of the warning hit me like a ton of bricks. It was like a slap in the face and I cried because they had no idea what we endured; the fear we had in Vietnam or the baggage of fear we brought home. I didn't expect to be the recipient of name calling, watching vicious sneers or being labeled a "Baby Killer." I wasn't a baby killer and hated the thoughts of the protestors. No baby or child was ever targeted, but the ravage of war takes its toll on all people.

While the protesters here in America were snug and warm in their houses and free of pain, we were being maimed by napalm. To this day, Vietnam Veterans are still being haunted by the visions of protestors, hung in no man's land where we are hated, and sunk into a quagmire of Government red tape. We don't exist. We are a forgotten man and woman.

Today, so many of the American Vietnam Veterans are physically and emotionally ill. We have never recovered. It has taken thirty five years for my government to acknowledge my Post Traumatic Stress Disorder. Thirty five damned long years! I want to know why. I want to know why government officials sit on their back sides and still do nothing to help us, while we go bankrupt in proving our illnesses. The government won't fess up to our needs. For the longest time, we were told a syndrome was a figment of our imagination. The word "syndrome" is nothing more than a label the doctors' place on the illnesses they can't or won't diagnose. A "disorder" has symptoms that can be proven.

I, Tommy J. Moon, am here to set the record straight. Post Traumatic Stress Disorder is a fact. I have been diagnosed with this debilitating emotional roller coaster ride—roller coaster ride with no ending, but to date have not received my full disability.

The letters I have written to Congressmen, explaining the need for my disability have fallen on deaf ears. I think the government has forgotten the war in Vietnam, just like they told us to forget we were ever over there. No living American Veteran or soldier who returns from war should have to convince a doctor they have nightmares, rage, fear, or uncontrollable outbursts or should be subjected to begging for assistance. God in Heaven, it is not fun to live or enjoyable to know your life is hanging by a thread—a thread so fragile all it takes is a snap to be institutionalized.

It does exist and I am living proof; I have lived with it every day of my life since I came home from Vietnam. The war is as fresh today as it was thirty five years ago. My mind magnifies the death and horror. I hear bombs exploding and agonizing screams of our men being ripped apart. Jets and helicopter roars set me into frenzy as I watch them pass above my head. Sirens set off a multitude of unbearable memories. I can't work at a job without some noise triggering thoughts of Vietnam.

My mind will veer off into a million directions while I am driving a car and before I realize what is happening, I might have gone through a red light. My current wife has to console me when I awake from horrific nightmares. She is my third wife; my loving and understanding wife. She will never know how much I appreciate and love her. My other two wives told me I was crazy and they could not live with a man skittish in seeing a simple butcher knife lying on the table.

For the longest time, I would clam up and not speak. Words were inside me but couldn't find an exit. I felt like a jigsaw puzzle, thrown on a table and scattered into a million pieces. No piece fit together. It was as though I was many persons, talking to one another trying to find an identity. One person would lash out into a rage, one would cry and the others would scream. I was not me. I was hung into thin air like a balloon, wanting desperately to jerk myself free from its tugging, powerful string. No direction I went could extract the explosive detonator lodged in my mind. The fuse was short and could erupt without provocation. All of this rage prevented me from sleeping.

God, I couldn't even sleep. I would stay awake as long as possible to avoid nightmares—those God awful nightmares waiting to engulf my mind. No body knows what it is like because they aren't experiencing it. It is terrifying. Telling the doctors about my plight doesn't seem to help. Medications help to a degree but it's not a cure-all. The depression raging inside me was and still is like a hot iron, searing me into an abyss—an abyss of darkness, anger, fears and uncontrollable fits tossing me into combat. Vietnam is all around me. My body is here in America but my mind is in Vietnam.

I've had people ask me why I am the way I am, reclusive and compulsive. They tell me I am paranoid and need to get a life and I need to leave Vietnam behind and move forward. If they understood and could see with my eyes, they wouldn't be so quick to judge.

People have no idea the torture I am going through. I don't like it anymore than they do. In fact, I hate it. I hate looking over my shoulder, seeing eyes in the trees; and wondering if those eyes are VC or the dead soldiers. People say I need to concentrate on the now and live for the moment. The battle scars prevent me from moving forward. I am hung in a time warp, shrouded by memories that won't die.

People who understand me are other Vietnam Veterans. They don't ask me why I can't do this or that. They know how I feel, although some can't talk about what they experienced. We don't have to talk. We understand the silence. We had to live silent in Vietnam, even with all the battles raging around us. We couldn't even light a cigarette without Charlie seeing us. A match or lighter was a signal to danger. One flick of light is all it took.

Some people remind me of the medals I earned and tell me to be proud of them. Sure, I earned medals. I have the National Defense Service Medal, Vietnam Cross of Gallantry with Palm, Good Conduct Medal, 3rd Award, Bronze Star Medal, Vietnam Service Medal with three Bronze Service Stars, and the Vietnam Campaign Medal with 60 Device. I also earned the Purple Heart but have never received it. Government red tape has kept me from receiving it. You know, all the medals in the world won't bring me back from things I witnessed, the things I endured, the hatred of my fellow man when I came home, or the torture I continue to live. Even as we live, we slowly die.

We, the American Vietnam Veterans, are the forgotten ones, the ones who "fell back" only to come forward and fall through the cracks of loneliness; from our beloved country, the United States of America."

Twelve

Several days later after speaking with Tommy J. Moon, I decided to find out more about the awful era of Vietnam. I was one of the millions of Americans who, for whatever reason, thought if I didn't think about the war, it would go away. But, it didn't, especially for the soldier's trapped so many miles away in a foreign land. I needed to learn more about Vietnam, even though it was many years later. It would be eye-opening. Trailing through archives of newspaper clippings, I found myself engrossed in the process of American Airlifts for those refugees who desperately wanted to vacate themselves of unwanted terror.

Why I chose this April 30th day to find out more on the subject, was beyond me. To tell you the truth, I was unaware of its magnitude but I would find out. It was the anniversary of, you might say, unfinished business for the Vietnamese people; a thirty year span from the end of the war. It was a revelation for me and made me realize what so many people did to free themselves from communism.

The dying Republic of Vietnam was in chaos. April 30, 1975, when the American soldiers began destroying documents, the world of the free Vietnam citizens turned into a free for all survival. Hundreds upon hundreds of Vietnamese nationals and citizens from other nations, allies to the American soldiers, were desperate to flee the country they loved.

It was more than any citizen could imagine; it was surreal to find your country overrun by radical personnel whose only aim in life was to irradiate simple living. The communists quickly surrounded the Vietnamese people; screened, classified and registered them as an enemy of the revolution. Many of the Vietnamese people were actually detained in concentration camps, forced and isolated into a miserable situation; parallel in kind to all the American armed military citizens of World War II. Communism raged like wildfire, erupting like acne on a teenager's face.

Absolutely no one could fathom what would come next. Graves of the fallen soldiers were desecrated by means of bulldozers; razed into heaps of nothingness, as though they never existed as human beings. Any means of communication were registered with the Socialist Republic of Vietnam. A simple typewriter, television or radio was outlawed as citizen ownership. It was non-existent. You had no rights, no civil liberties—nothing.

As my mind wandered through tons of material on the subject of Vietnam, I was proud to know I was an American citizen. Pondering the aspect of living without freedom or the right to live where religious beliefs are not allowed, sent shivers down my spine. It made me understand the plight of so many Vietnamese wanting to flee their homeland in search of better things.

In my minds eye, I could visualize the air lifts. Panicked civilians running for their lives, leaving all they owned for a taste of freedom. Families ripped apart in order to secure a livelihood for survival must have been their only option. They scurried toward American airplanes begging to be released from torture, mayhem and death. It would be a safe haven in America. What must have been flowing within their minds could only be obtained through escape.

The United States of America became the refugee center of the world. A surge of one hundred twenty nine thousand Indochina refugees entered through the Immigration and Naturalization Service on April 22, 1975.

Many areas throughout the Untied States were servicing and housing these victims of war. I can only surmise the problems they faced; foreign foods to their digestive tracts, a language barrier, no money, no jobs, no family support and a country apprehensive to accept them. After all, the American forces had been to Vietnam. Many of our young men and women were killed in their homeland due to an undeclared war and now our country was accepting them with open arms. For some Veterans, it was too much. While the Veterans did without necessary medical attention and a warm welcome from the American citizens, the Vietnamese people were garnering what our returning soldiers needed most.

Although it took awhile, because hatred ran rampant, attitudes changed among some Americans but it was a long haul for the newly arrived people. Trapped inside barracks chosen by the government, many Vietnamese people harbored fear. How would they survive? Through translators, they were able to learn English and learn trades to see them through hard times. The majority of Vietnamese men and women had the determination to establish a work force, working several jobs each day. For them it was not an eight hour shift, where the average American goes home after a long days work, but instead, an eight hour work day turned into all-nighters. Most of their money returned to Vietnam to support families left behind.

~ * ~

I had enough of rummaging archives. No, I didn't learn in two days what I needed to understand Vietnam but my eyes were opened to a different belief. None of this would bring back my father but it did allow me release. My attitude toward the quiet Vietnamese people had changed. They were not here to cause pain toward us, nor did they want to inflict their way of living. All they wanted was true peace. A peace they could not have under the rule of communism. Reading all the articles left me with a profound change of heart. I couldn't sit in judgment of how people felt about Vietnam or even why the war had to be. It was a tragic thing, just like any previous war and even the war in Iraq. As long as there are people, there will be some kind of war raging…because we are human and have human frailties. One thing I did learn was respect, in that, respect is earned…not demanded.

Dad died to help them on their home ground even though he probably didn't understand it any more than I do today. His death was not in vain for the Vietnamese people. I realized how proud I was of him. If he could do such a brave thing on foreign soil, he would have done the same thing here, if he had lived.

Thirteen

Melissa and I didn't talk much about Ralph and I hadn't had the opportunity to tell her about Tommy. Well, maybe I did have an opportunity but her frame of mind probably wouldn't have been open to another round of Vietnam stories. I wanted to tell her what Tommy told me and let her read what I had written. I also wanted to tell her about the Vietnamese people and what they, as a nation went through.

Neither one of us wanted to broach the subject but deep down, we knew the time would come to talk. It was necessary to continue the healing process. There was a lot I wanted to say and the only way to do it was blurt out the words. Today would be the day for our talk, because we were scheduled to start fencing in Mom's property so I could make her house mine and Patches. The money she set aside for fencing my yard would be put to use and I didn't think she would mind if I chose to fence her yard instead of mine. It was a larger yard and Patches needed room to roam.

Although I didn't really need the money, I opted to rent my house for additional income and set the money aside for repairs for both houses. I contacted the local fence installer and told him I would meet him at the house within the hour. Loading up my car with tools I might need to assist him, Patches and I set off to pick up Melissa.

Backing out of the driveway, I did a once over of my house and yard. It's not something I do on a regular basis but today left me speechless. Routinely, I go through the garage into the kitchen and very seldom use the front door, unless someone rings the bell.

Stopping the car and rolling down the window so Patches wouldn't get hot, I ventured toward the porch. I couldn't believe my eyes. There, in the confines, lay at least one hundred and fifty teddy bears. Some had notes attached to them stating "I hope this is your bear" while others simply lay there waiting to be picked up and cuddled. My mouth gaped and I stood in awe of so many generous people wanting to help me find Patch Dimple. It looked like a toy store without the children, except for me. I was the child whose dream was being fulfilled, at least to a point.

Unfortunately, none of the teddy bears was Patch Dimple and he was still at large, unwilling to come forth to ease my pain. What was I going to do with all these stuffed bears? I couldn't return them to the givers so I decided to donate them to the children's ward at the hospital.

I phoned Melissa and asked her to please meet the man who was to erect the fence at Mom's house. When I told her what I was going to do, she told me not to get into such a rush because she had a surprise for me. Not knowing what she meant, I shoved bears inside the trunk, on the seats and floorboard of my car and headed toward Mom's house. Patches and I barely had room to maneuver. Melissa told me she was already there and waiting on me and so was another two hundred bears.

Bears were everywhere! Under trees, inside the mail box, on the front porch and propped along the side of the house. Mom's house looked like a colorful candy factory of Gummy Bears. A few of them were very large, the kind you get on Valentine's Day and the color of bright red hearts. Most of them were brown and more manageable in size.

There was no way I could stuff all these other bears in my car without doing myself bodily harm. Although none of them remotely looked like my lost bear, I was overcome by the generosity of so many persons out to do a good deed.

We sat on the lawn wondering how we could transport three hundred and fifty bears to the hospital. My car was already stuffed to the brim and couldn't accommodate another fluffy critter. The neighbors, curious to see what was transpiring within their peaceful haven, were gathering to see all the early Christmas presents.

Out of the blue, a newspaper reporter strolled up snapping pictures right and left. I was astonished and somewhat baffled why so many people were eager to learn about Patch Dimple.

The reporter spoke with me for about an hour, delaying my quest in erecting the much needed fence but for the first time, I was eager to talk about Patch Dimple and why retrieving him was so important to me.

I learned, from the reporter, that the ad I placed in the newspaper touched many hearts. The phone lines at the Centennial were lit up like a Christmas tree from persons eager to replace my beloved Patch Dimple. It was not customary, I was told, to release addresses of people whose ads appear in classifieds but under the circumstances, my plea left the Centennial in a quandary. Release my address or have tons of bears show up on the newspaper's doorstep. Letters sent to the Centennial had my name in bold letters and were delivered to me by this 'eager for a story' reporter. It was more than I ever dreamed possible.

Then my mind wandered to Kenny Sevenstar because trying to find him was a dead end search. My letters to Kenny had been returned to me and the internet had been no help. It was as though he dropped off the face of the earth. I had no way of knowing that one of the letters the reporter delivered to me would be from Kenny. It would be the icing on the cake.

Before the reporter left, he engaged a transport service to carry the happy little bears to the hospital. His last words to me were, "Read the paper tomorrow because this will be the front page lead."

Dumbfounded is hardly a word to describe how I was feeling. It was more like I had just been handed the key to the city and didn't know which lock to turn. When all the commotion died down, I thought things would return to normal. I was wrong.

While Melissa and I walked around in a daze, the fence installer was walking the perimeter of the yard. Several days prior, I had marked off the distance with a can of bright orange spray paint. All the installer needed to do was measure the area for the metal posts and begin using a post-hole digger. I would prepare the concrete for each metal structure and cut down on the time spent for manual labor. Melissa was to begin painting the interior of the house, and Patches would do her normal thing; sleep...or so I thought. This day would be like no other day; it would bring surprises of all kinds.

We introduced ourselves, shook hands and began our work. Half way into the day, sweat pouring off our brows and hungry, the installer and I went inside for a quick lunch and respite from the sun. We sat on the floor just inside the kitchen door, drinking Gatorade, woofing down our sandwiches and talking about ordinary things. Somehow the conversation turned toward the government, a subject I didn't normally broach with casual acquaintances. It wasn't because I didn't enjoy a lively conversation but in most instances tempers flared when two minds did not agree upon the topic. Before I knew what the avenue our conversation would take he piped up. "I'm surprised I am not dead."

Startled with his outburst I looked at him. "What did you say?"

"I'm surprised I am not dead."

"Why on earth would you say such a thing?"

"I have a piece of shrapnel in my mediastinum."

I had no clue as to what he was saying and could only assume he was lucid. "All right, if you say so."

"You don't get it do you?"

"No, man, I don't. If you want me to understand what you are saying, talk to me in language I can grasp. I know what shrapnel is but the mediastinum is Greek to me."

"I got it in the war. Hell, I didn't even know it was there until I had an x-ray. I thought I had lung cancer. You know, pain and all. All these years I have been lugging around a piece of metal the size of my little finger."

I yelled, "Melissa, come in here a minute."

"What do you need? I only have a minute before this paint dries on my roller."

"What is a mediastinum?"

"It's the space separating the two pleural sacs of the chest."

"What? Melissa, tell me in plain English."

"You have your heart on the left side, lungs in front of the heart...one lung on each side of the body. You do understand what I am saying, don't you?"

"Yeah, I get a portion of what you are saying. Where is the mediastinum?"

"It's between all of those organs...a space extending from the breastbone back to the thoracic vertebrae and down toward the diaphragm. The lungs are not contained in this area. Why do you want to know where the mediastinum is located?"

"Mike just told me he has shrapnel in his mediastinum and I was curious how he could walk around all these years without knowing it was there."

"It's not so unusual. I've seen many men with pieces of metal in their bodies. They come in for surgery and the doctors find it. You can't expect the doctors to find all the shrapnel in time of war. They usually patch the men up as well as possible and ship them back into combat. If you are satisfied, may I go back to finish painting?"

"Be my guest. Melissa, have you seen Patches?"

"She was here a few minutes ago. She's probably curled up on the mat in the living room."

Mike piped up again. "Are you talking about the German shepherd?"

"Yeah, I am. Why do you ask? She's my sidekick."

"Well, I saw your sidekick tearing up the lattice work in the front yard. I shooed her off thinking it was a stray."

I threw down my sandwich and ran to the front of the yard. I screamed for Melissa to help. "Oh, good grief! Patches, is at it again. What in thunder am I going to do with her? I tried to coax her out from under the house but this time she growled at me."

"Todd, until you crawl under the house to see what she has treed, this will continue. Patches apparently likes whatever is under there."

"God, I hate crawl spaces!"

"You didn't mind it when you were small."

"If you haven't noticed, I'm not small and I only have one good leg." I went inside the house, took off my prosthesis and slammed my crutch under my arm and yelled, "I hate this damned thing!"

Melissa placed an old, paint spattered drop cloth on the ground and I maneuvered myself into position. Jerking off the remainder of un-chewed lattice, I gritted my teeth and proceeded under the house. I have to admit I was angry at myself for not finding out Patches secret the first time her excursion left me exhausted.

"I am going to need more than this dinky little flash light. Go next door to Mr. Dixon's and see if he has a work light."

"What? I didn't understand a word you said."

"I said...." Oh bull, she probably wouldn't know what I needed. I was going to have to craw out of this spider infested, dank old hole and get it myself.

Crawling from under the house, I saw Melissa grinning from ear to ear. "My word, Todd, don't you look handsome? Why I haven't seen as much dirt on a face since you were small."

"Don't get cute with me. I guess you think it's funny seeing a one legged, grown man squirm through dirt, grit and spider's webs don't you?"

"As a matter of fact, yes, I do. You have a boyish look to your face and I love it. What were you telling me to do? You sounded muffled."

"I wanted you to go next door and borrow a wide beamed light from my neighbor."

Melissa smiled and held up the work light. "You mean this thing?"

"Dad-gum it, Melissa. Why didn't you just hand me the blasted thing when I yelled at you?"

"I just wanted to see how angry you could get. Ever since I came home, you've never gotten irate and I only wanted to see if you were for real."

"What?"

"Oh, I knew you were different but to tell you the truth, I thought you might be putting on an act."

"Act? What are you saying? Do I look like I am acting? I am sweating my head off, digging around under here for a dog whose idea of fun is chewing off lattice work and you think I am acting? I am not acting, Melissa. Right now I am madder than a wet hen."

"You don't understand, Todd. If this is the only way

you appear when you are annoyed, then I have hit the jackpot."

I snickered. "Melissa, you beat all. Do you know it? Hand me the blasted light so I can find out what Patches finds so intriguing."

Positioning myself on the ground, I made my way under the house. The extension cord on the light became tangled around the concrete pillar supporting the house and I became more frustrated than ever. It seemed like an omen. Perhaps I was not supposed to find out the secret. As I jerked on the cord, a familiar voice yelled, "Hey, Todd, what are you doing under there? Need some help?"

"Tommy, what are you doing here?"

"Oh, I was passing by and thought I would see what the commotion was all about. Actually, Todd, our conversation at Denny's the other day kept running through my mind. Being here is not an accident. I want you to have these pictures, if you want them."

"Pictures?"

"Yeah, they are of my tour in Vietnam. I was young and handsome in the photos but it was thirty some odd years ago. I thought the pictures might come in handy. I don't have many."

"I would love to put them with my collection of letters from my Dad. I wrote down what you told me and it is mighty impressive information. One of these days, I will make a shadow box full of mementos. Your story and pictures will be included."

"Well, you didn't answer me. Would you like some help under there?"

"Just untangle the cord for me. There's no need for you to get all dirty. But if something grabs me, get your butt under here."

Melissa and Mike had noticed I had been gone for some time and came out to see what kept me from resuming work on the fence. I was glad because Melissa would meet Tommy and it would be a way to introduce to her the ordeal Tommy encountered in the war and give me an opportunity to broach the death of Ralph.

Looking around I saw Patches. She was hunkered in the north corner of the house, near the concrete pillar. She was near a ledge I used as a hiding place for secrets. Memories flooded over me revealing a time and place of my youth.

After Dad died, I would make sure no one was watching and descend to the catacombs, the darkest place I could find to hide my tears and write personal notes to him. There was no way I could give Dad my scribbles or express to him my fears and emotional problems but it was a release for me. Seeing Patches lay near my quiet place soothed my childhood nightmares and left me with a supreme calm.

"Patches, how did you know this was my place? Girl, you are truly a remarkable dog. What are you so enamored with, Patches? Move over and let me see." I brushed away a mound of dirt and nearly had a heart attack. My hands were shaking so hard I could barely maneuver the light. I let out a scream—a loud whooping scream.

"Melissa! Help me, please, help me."

I could hear Melissa, Mike and Tommy scramble to the opening of the crawl space. Melissa's voice was panicked. "Todd, are you hurt? Where are you?"

"I'm at the corner of the house."

"Which corner, Todd?"

"Go to the north corner and pull off the lattice. Hurry!"

"Oh, my God! Mike, he must be hurt. Find something and pull off the rest of the underpinning. Tommy will you find my purse, get the keys and unlock the trunk of my car. There is a first aid kit in the trunk."

Hearing them tear away the wood was a relief

because there was no way I would ever get my precious find from under the house. Patches was barking and I was crying, knowing the key to my past was unfolding right before my eyes—all because of Patches.

"Todd, how badly are you hurt?" cried Melissa.

"Oh, I'm not hurt. I just can't get back to the small opening with what I've found."

"Man," Tommy shouted. "We thought you were dying. You had us scared to death. Get your lousy butt out here."

Patches squirmed through the cavity and I shoved the rusty tin box from its hiding place. It took a few minutes for me to extract myself from the dirty hole but those few minutes felt like hours. To think I had my childhood within reach, to peer back in time was a joy beyond my wildest dreams. My excitement spilled over with a thunderous, "Halleluiah!"

We gathered around as though I had found the lost Ark. In reality, I had, but to them it was just an old dirty, rusty box. To Patches, it was a symbol or a larger sample of the tin box I used to hide her rubber ball. Perhaps Patches thought the container held the key to her enjoyment. Whatever anyone felt, I could never explain how my heart swelled with joy. I could only show them the contents.

The hinges to the box were rusty and the clasp did not want to relinquish its hold, but a screwdriver and hammer convinced the box to unleash the contents. The lid popped open and there lay Patch Dimple, resurrected from thirty some odd years. I gently reached inside and retrieved my beloved companion—a companion whose only lot in life was to guide me through a bout of depression, loneliness and fear.

I held Patch Dimple up in the air, and then placed him to my face. I hoped there would be a faint scent of Dad. I'm not sure if there was but my mind replayed those last days when we were together. Through tears, I placed my large hand inside the cavity of Patch Dimple's stomach. As I turned my hand over, Dad's Purple Heart plopped lovingly inside my palm. The letters I hid were like frankincense and myrrh, a precious gift known only to me. My emotions were at an all time high and I collapsed into a heap, sobbing. Melissa, with her loving attitude knelt with me and wept.

Tommy and Mike were like soldiers—soldiers standing guard over a wounded comrade. Helping me up from the ground, they escorted me to the house, all the while understanding the enormity of the day. Melissa picked up the old box and carried it to the kitchen placing it on the cabinet. As we sat down on the linoleum, the box fell, creating a rusty blob on the floor. However, as Melissa swept up the debris, a small envelope slid across the linoleum.

Through swollen eyes Melissa looked at Todd. "I believe you dropped one of your letters."

I took it from her, turned it over to read Dad's handwriting but it wasn't from him. The outside of the letter read: "Todd." Curious to find out what the letter contained, I opened the flap. As the folded letter unfurled, a one hundred dollar bill fell into my lap. "What in the world is this? I don't know anything about this letter. I didn't put it inside the box."

"For crying out loud, man, read it. Don't keep us in suspense," yelled Mike. "Do you realize this day has been one surprise after another? Teddy bears, newspaper reporter, the fence is not up and we are all sitting on the floor crying like little kids? Read the letter!"

~ * ~

Dear Todd,

If you are reading this, then I know you have Patch Dimple, the letters you hid and your Dad's Purple Heart. I was going to purchase this old box from your Mother at the garage sale but realized it should not be sold.

When I looked inside the box and found what it contained, I cried. These items weren't meant to be sold, so while no one was watching, I pushed it under the house. When Kenny Sevenstar saw what I was doing, he started to yell. He thought I was trying to steal your belongings. It took a few minutes to convince him he needed to be my partner in this deed. He promised he would crawl under the house and hide the box where you would find it and keep his mouth shut. Well, a fifty dollar payoff to him sealed the deal.

I know your mom will never take these hundred dollars from me, so in order to help her, I have to be devious. She is so proud she would never allow me to give her money unless she worked overtime at the clinic. She works too hard as it is and doesn't need to feel obligated to me in any way.

Will you please give your Mother this money and promise never to tell her where you got it? Another thing, put Patch Dimple in a safe place so you will always have these memories.

Your friend,
Doc Crowder

"Well, I'll be. All these years have passed and Patch Dimple held more secrets than I imagined. Mom thought she sold my prized possession."

"Didn't you ever go back under the house after the garage sale?" Mike asked.

"No. It had grown old and I was getting too large to shimmy between the dirt and the foundation. Besides, my interest turned toward girls and I didn't want my clothes to get dirty."

Melissa grinned. "I remember."

I chuckled. "Yeah, you and half the neighbors. I remember when Mom found us together under an old tent."

Melissa slapped Todd on the back. "Don't tell the whole lot of our secrets."

"Ah, go on, Todd. Tell us about it," grinned Tommy. "You know you want to relive old times. What were you two doing inside the tent?"

Melissa blushed. "We weren't doing anything."

"Yes we were. I was trying to kiss you and you were giggling. You thought it was funny and I didn't."

"It was funny. You had an Eskimo Pie smeared all over your face. You were sticky and it looked like you had been wallowing in pig mud."

Tommy laughed too. "What happened when your Mom intervened?"

"She didn't do much, except yell to the heavens that I should know better. It was hot outside, like it is today, and the neighbors were sitting in lawn chairs. Before I knew what was happening, they were standing there clapping their hands yelling, "Way to go, Todd."

"I was so embarrassed I ran all the way home. I knew if the neighbors told my mom that Todd was trying to kiss me, I wouldn't be able to look them in the eye. You know something? She never did say a word."

"Well, you were the lucky one, Melissa. Mom read me the riot act when she got me inside the house. I think she thought it would make me want to do other things."

"Maybe that is why she turned the water hose on you when you tried to do it again. You guys should have seen Todd. Water was shooting up his nose."

"Melissa. You just told me not to tell everything I know, so you can do likewise."

She blushed again. "Well, I don't know about you three men but I have painting to do and the fence is not getting installed. We've had enough excitement for one day, now it is time to get our work finished. Coffee and lunch is over. Get to it."

Somehow we managed to complete our days work and I was ecstatic. The newspaper reporter, eager to find out more about Patch Dimple, returned to do another interview. This time it wasn't to snap pictures of donated teddy bears but to show the world the actual picture of Patch Dimple and the story surrounding his captivity for so many years. My life had managed to pull together a full circle. It was time to move forward and close the gate.

Fourteen

It was 7:30 p.m. on this Memorial Day—a day of remembrances. American Flag's were proudly displayed on houses in the town square and lined the National Cemetery. It was a fitting example of our heritage.

As I looked toward the east, a faint pastel rainbow could be seen on the horizon. I had been sitting on the pitted concrete bench the entire day, unaware of the light rain falling around me. Perhaps it was a prophecy of good things to come or a symbol of washing away the years of pain. I felt cleansed; a new man with a new beginning. My conversation with Dad felt good.

So many things spilled from me, it was hard to contain my composure. My heart felt full of joy knowing at long last, peace had come over me. The ton of bricks, aptly called emotional turmoil, I carried around for thirty years had been lifted from my chest.

I took a deep breath of fresh air and stood up. Surprisingly, I hadn't been alone through these hours of talking to Dad. Other people were having visits with their loved ones but I was oblivious to their presence. Flowers adorned tomb stones placed in close proximity to Dad and Mom's graves but in my state of mind, I was alone with him…void of any passerby's footsteps or voice. For me, it was a time to renew our son and father relationship.

From a slow moving automobile exiting the cemetery, I heard the beautiful voice of Bette Midler singing a familiar song, *Wind Beneath My Wings*. The sound of the lyrics floated throughout the cemetery, giving rise to its patriotic theme. *"Did you ever know you were my hero, and everything I'd like to be?"* The music faded as the car slowly made its way out of sight. It left goose bumps on my skin. I longed to hear more of the song.

It was time. Time for me to exit the gated community—a community of kindred spirits. It wasn't lonely anymore and I wasn't afraid to face the future and what it held. I had come full circle, once again, in talking with Dad. It might sound strange but I knew Dad understood what I had been feeling, the fears overtaking me. It was subtle, a gentle gesture nudging me to leave.

There was one thing left for me to do. Walking toward the car, tears flowed with the realization of what I was about to do. Pride swelled within me and the urge to shout had to be contained. Lifting the precious cargo from the trunk was the final salute to my fallen hero.

Quietly, I placed flowers upon Mom's grave, told her I loved her and I had something special to do. I knelt on my knees caressing the final goodbye and whispered, *"This is for you, Dad. It's the only thing I can give you to let you know how proud I am of you. Mr. McGuire, the gatekeeper, told me it would be safe to leave him here. It's Patch Dimple, Dad. You remember Patch Dimple don't you? He's a little worn and tattered but he reflects your talents—a warrior full of love and compassion. I put him in a Plexiglas container so he would be out of the elements. It's my way of letting you know how much I love you. Patch Dimple was my source of comfort and now I want you to be comforted by him.*

He will watch over you, Dad, like he watched over me when I was small. Your Purple Heart is in a glass case at my house, along with the letters you wrote to me. By the way,

Dad, there's a letter addressed to you inside his pouch. I know you won't ever be able to read it but its there, just like I will be in the future to talk. Next time I come to see you, I will bring Melissa, your daughter-in-law. She's a great lady and you would love her, just the way I do."

As I walked away to return home, the letter I had written to Dad gently fell from the pouch as though he was reading the words I had written. It began: *Dad, Did I ever tell you, you were my hero and everything I'd like to be...?*

Joyce L. Rapier

About Joyce

Joyce Rapier resides in Arkansas and is the author of WINDY JOHN'S ME 'N TUT, WINDY JOHN'S RAINBOW AND THE POT O' GOLD and WHISPER MY NAME. Her short story, HIDDEN WINGS, was published in the 2005 CHICKEN SOUP FOR THE FATHER DAUGHTER'S SOUL. Several of her short stories have been included in anthologies. To find the latest news, you may visit Joyce's web site at
www.authorsden.com/joycelrapier

Visit our website for our growing catalogue of quality books.
www.ezppublishing.com

High Risk
by
Jane Toombs

ISBN: 189726139X

Three women flee through mountains that took their friend's life earlier. Now a violent storm rages while a deadly killer trails them...

Send cheque or money order for $16.95 USD
+$4.00 S & H ($20.95) to:
Champagne Books
#35069-4604 37 St SW
Calgary, AB Canada T3E 7C7

Name:	
Address:	
City/State:	ZIP:
Country:	

**From award winning author,
Lori Derby Bingley**

One Man. Six Women. And a Fraternity filled with brothers who will do anything to keep their secrets.

Send cheque or money order for $9.95 USD
+$4.00 S & H ($13.95) to:
Champagne Books
#35069-4604 37 St SW
Calgary, AB Canada T3E 7C7

Name:	
Address:	
City/State:	ZIP:
Country:	

Joyce L. Rapier

Printed in the United States
64893LVS00001B/67-75

9 781897 261873